# "She really is the sweetest baby I've ever seen..."

"I like to think she takes after me," Hank said in a teasing voice.

"I think she's really fortunate to have you, Hank," Sage murmured. "Your devotion to her is crystal clear."

"I think we're blessed to have one another," Hank said, warmed by Sage's words. He reached out and gently took Lulu from Sage's arms. A little sigh escaped Sage's lips as he made the transfer.

Being so close to her was a dangerous thing, as he'd discovered earlier at the diner. The more time he spent in her presence, the more appealing she seemed. As it was, he found himself thinking about her at random moments during the day.

All of his professional instincts were warning him that something was off with Sage, yet his heart was pulling him in her direction.

Despite his firm resolve to have nothing to do with the beautiful schoolteacher, Hank was having a difficult time ignoring the yearning sensation he felt every time she was in his orbit...

**Belle Calhoune** grew up in a small town in Massachusetts. Married to her college sweetheart, she is raising two lovely daughters in Connecticut. A dog lover, she has one mini poodle and a chocolate Lab. Writing for the Love Inspired line is a dream come true. Working at home in her pajamas is one of the best perks of the job. Belle enjoys summers in Cape Cod, traveling and reading.

# Her Secret Alaskan Family

## Belle Calhoune

HARLEQUIN® LOVE INSPIRED®

LOVE INSPIRED BOOKS

Recycling programs
for this product may
not exist in your area.

ISBN-13: 978-1-335-48790-2

Her Secret Alaskan Family

www.Harlequin.com

**Printed in U.S.A.**

He healeth the broken in heart, and bindeth up their wounds. He telleth the number of the stars; he calleth them all by their name.
—*Psalm* 147:3–4

For my parents, Anne and Fred Bell.
For everything. For always.

## Acknowledgments

For my husband, Randy, and my daughters,
Sierra and Amber. For always cheering me on
and understanding that writing
is an important part of me.

To my editor, Emily Rodmell,
for being so receptive to this story
and allowing me to write it.

# Chapter One

"Welcome to the last frontier," Sage Duncan murmured as she walked to the bow of the ferry and looked out across the breathtaking waters of Kachemak Bay.

Despite her frayed nerves, Sage was able to appreciate the raw beauty of her surroundings. She took a deep breath and inhaled the crisp Alaskan air. Snow-covered mountains rose up to greet her. A bird swooped down toward the water, then emerged a few seconds later with a fish in its mouth. Sage shook her head at the stunning sights unfolding before her eyes. The vista was spectacular. It was like nothing she had ever seen before in her life.

In her wildest dreams she had never envisioned herself traveling to this magnificent land. It had always seemed so out of reach, like a faraway constellation in the heavens.

She shivered and wrapped her arms around her middle. This Alaskan climate was a far cry from back home in Florida where heat and humidity reigned. Sage couldn't remember the last time she had seen snow, but as a little girl she had fantasized about catching snowflakes on her tongue and sledding down snowy mountains in the wintertime.

Sage shook off those long-ago memories. She hadn't traveled all this way to Owl Creek, Alaska, in order to live out her childhood dreams. Her reasons for coming here were complicated, and hurt bubbled up inside her as the reality of her situation kicked her in the gut.

Her mother's death two months ago had changed her life in so many ways. With her dying breath, Jane Duncan had made a startling confession to Sage. Months later and she was still processing the revelation. According to her mother, Sage had been stolen as a baby from her birth family. Right after Jane had uttered those shocking words she had died, leaving Sage with a hundred burning questions. Who was she? Who were her real family? Why had Jane Duncan committed such a horrific act as kidnapping somebody else's child?

Digging through her mother's belongings had turned up old newspaper clippings about a three-month-old baby who had been taken from her crib in the middle of the night, never to be seen again. Goose bumps had popped up on her arms when she'd come across a photo with the word MISSING written in bold black print on the flyer. There were two pictures side by side—one of a baby girl and the other a pretty teenager. The words *age enhanced* were written beneath the image. The girl had looked a little bit like her. Similar features. Same age. Even the same birth month.

A search on the internet had turned up even more information. If what she suspected turned out to be true, her real name was Lily North. Her family—the

Norths—were the owners of the North Star Chocolate Company. Her parents still lived in Owl Creek and they had never stopped looking for her or praying for her return. Her image had even been plastered on milk cartons back when she was an infant.

Which was why, in order to seek out those answers, she had traveled to this southern portion of Alaska and booked herself into a cozy bed-and-breakfast in Owl Creek for a period of six weeks.

Sage felt a solid presence next to her as she looked out toward land. She turned to her right. The man standing a few feet away from her was handsome. He was looking in her direction, his eyes focused on her like laser beams. With sandy-colored hair and turquoise blue eyes, he had a rugged appearance. A shiny gold badge sat on his chest.

He quirked his mouth. "Let me guess. You're Lily North, aren't you?"

Sage's knees threatened to give way beneath her, and her heart began to beat like thunder inside her chest. Why had she thought she could get away with this?

"Wh-what are you talking about?" she asked, wondering how in the world this stranger knew her true purpose for being in Owl Creek.

He let out a chuckle. His features immediately went from attractive to downright spectacular. "Sorry. Just a bad joke. Our little town has been inundated with women claiming to be the missing North baby." He frowned at her. "Surely you've heard about the case?"

"Just a little bit," she hedged. "I'm not from Alaska,

but I recall seeing some news coverage a few weeks ago back home."

"It's the twenty-fifth anniversary of the kidnapping so it's been plastered all over the news and on the internet," he explained. "Every scam artist from here to Toledo has been trying to fleece the family by pretending to be Lily. It's been going on for years but lately it's gotten out of hand. I was born and bred in Owl Creek so I've grown up hearing about the case." His expression turned somber. "In a way it's always cast a shadow over the town."

"Do you know them? The Norths?" she asked, her curiosity getting the best of her. She wanted to learn everything she possibly could about them. Were they kind people? Had the kidnapping taken all the joy out of their lives? Had they moved past it?

"Sure do," he said amiably. "They're good people. Connor North is one of my best friends. And they make some of the best chocolate you'll ever taste." He stuck out his hand. "By the way, I'm Hank Crawford. Town sheriff."

She reached out and shook his hand. "So that explains the fancy badge," she said with a smile. "I'm Sage Duncan."

"Are you a tourist? We get a lot of them in our little town, but not usually in the winter. The weather is pretty intimidating for those who aren't used to it."

She wrinkled her nose. "I suppose you could call me a tourist. I teach second grade back home in Florida and I'm on leave for a few months. I've always wanted to visit Alaska, and I do adore chocolate," she said. "Call me crazy, but I'm looking forward to some wintry weather."

"You'll need a winter parka and some insulated boots for winter in Owl Creek. Otherwise you'll freeze," he advised, giving her attire the once-over. He was wearing a hunter green parka and a dark pair of cords. Sage had the feeling her clothing hadn't passed muster. Her decision to travel to Alaska had been made rather quickly. She'd taken a leave of absence and booked her airline tickets as well as the bed-and-breakfast before she could change her mind and chicken out. As a Floridian she didn't own many cold-weather clothes, so she'd done a little shopping online and stocked up on a few sweaters, hats and pants. She looked down at her boots. They were suede with fringes on them. Hardly fitting for the Alaskan climate. She hoped this little village had clothing stores and winter gear so she could round out her wardrobe.

"Thanks," she said, unwilling to offer any more information to Sheriff Crawford. She had already said too much, and he was the last person whose suspicions she wanted to arouse.

"Well, we're about to dock. It was nice to meet you, Sage," he said with a grin. "In a town as small as Owl Creek, I'm sure we'll be seeing each other."

Sage nodded and murmured goodbye as she watched the sheriff walk away from her. His gait was confident and strong. She let out a ragged sigh. Hank Crawford was no doubt the handsomest man she'd met in quite some time. But she wasn't in town to meet good-looking men. Not by a long shot. Sage had traveled all this way in order to scope out the people she believed might be her birth family. There was power in no one knowing she might actually be Lily North. She wouldn't have anyone questioning her motives or digging into her background.

She would have time to decide what to do.

At this point she had no idea whether or not she would reveal her identity to the North family. Doing so might cause a world of legal trouble for Eric Duncan, the man who she had called father for the last twenty-five years. According to her dad, he'd been in the dark about her mother's actions up until her dying day. Sadly, he had never addressed certain irregularities in Sage's adoption, which could make it appear as if he'd known the truth all along. Eric had asserted he'd never had any knowledge about her being kidnapped. He'd believed that her birth parents had abandoned her. From what he'd disclosed to Sage it was evident that her adoption hadn't been legal. Having just lost her mother, Sage couldn't imagine losing her father as well if the North family decided to file charges against him for being her mother's accomplice.

Sage clenched her fists at her sides. She would do anything in her power to protect him.

Hank hadn't meant to talk to the beautiful woman on the ferry, but there had been something about Sage Duncan that had tugged at him. She had looked so sad staring out across the water, and he had wanted to make her smile. Instead, he'd made himself look like a goofball.

Hank winced. He had made the corny joke about her being Lily North, which had landed with a little bit of a thud. Sage had looked at him with horror radiating from her eyes. She probably thought it was in bad form to make a joke about a missing person.

What Sage didn't know was that two years ago Hank had fallen for a woman named Theresa Bennett. They had gone out for a few months, during which time he had grown fond of Theresa. A short while later he had discovered she was nothing more than a fraud. A beautiful con artist bent on extorting money from his friends the Norths by pretending to be their missing child. Theresa had made a prize fool out of him. He imagined people were joking about how she'd pulled the wool over the eyes of a member of law enforcement. Just thinking about it made Hank's face flush with embarrassment.

So, in actuality he had really been laughing at his own stupidity when he'd cracked the joke about Sage being Lily North. Theresa had already burned him on that front. Once bitten, twice shy. He wasn't going down that road again.

He owed it to his daughter, Addie, to use more discretion when it came to romance. Hank let out a grunt. He really hadn't dated since that adorable little charmer had come into his life. And although the whole Theresa fiasco still stung a bit, she'd also given him his daughter. He would always be grateful. Addie's birth had led him straight to his relationship with Christ.

It wasn't as if he was dying of loneliness or anything. Being a full-time father and town sheriff kept him very busy. In his experience, romance brought nothing but upheaval, and he had resigned himself to the fact that he wasn't going to walk through life with a soul mate. Not everyone got the happy ending.

His thoughts veered to his best friend, Gabriel Lawson. Gabe had found out the hard way about shattered dreams when his fiancée had taken off two days before their wedding. No, sir. Hank didn't need someone to hand him his heart on a platter.

As the ferry glided into dock and the captain announced their arrival, Hank did his best not to look for Sage. The boat wasn't crowded with passengers, and in her cherry-red jacket it wouldn't take much effort to spot her. But he really didn't need any distractions, especially ones with jet-black hair, tiny freckles dotting their cheeks and doe-brown eyes flecked with gold.

Just as the thought popped into his head, Hank spotted Sage struggling with an oversize piece of luggage. Despite his vow not to get involved, he found himself walking over toward her. His mother had raised him to be a gentleman after all.

"Can I help you with your bags?" he asked Sage, admiring her pluck in attempting to wield the baggage.

She immediately let go of the piece of luggage. Her shoulders sagged with relief. "Thanks for asking. I may have overstuffed it a bit," she admitted. "When in doubt, pack everything you can. It's far better to have too much clothing than too little."

Hank felt the corners of his mouth twitching with merriment. The suitcase was nearly as big as the woman herself. He led the way off the ferry and down the pier. Once they reached the pickup area, he deposited the luggage on the ground. Although he wanted to ask her if she had a ride and where she was staying, Hank felt he might be overstepping if he did so. A few minutes ago it was as if a curtain had come down over her face when they had been speaking. As a law enforcement officer, he had been trained to watch facial expressions and body language. She had seemed a bit closed off.

However, Hank was far less adept at picking up on signals from females. His romantic past still hung over him like a dark cloud.

Sage was appealing to him and he didn't quite know how to handle the situation. Judging by her ring finger, she was single. It was a rare occasion when he felt such an attraction at first sight. But it didn't matter what he felt. He needed to focus on the lessons he'd learned in the past from his ex-girlfriend. He had no intention of making himself vulnerable again. Now that he was a man of faith, his entire life had transformed. Finding God made him want to be a better man.

Hank couldn't wait to see his little girl. He had only been away for twenty-four hours at a law enforcement summit in Homer, but he'd missed her terribly. Being a single dad wasn't easy, but Addie had quickly wormed her way into his heart.

His daughter had come into his life unexpectedly when Theresa passed away in a car accident in Kodiak. Hank hadn't even known of the little girl's existence when she had been thrust into his life eight months ago. After a bit of a rocky start, he and Addie had developed an incredible bond. Although he had long ago given up on romantic love, Hank knew without a shadow of a doubt that his daughter was the the most precious blessing God could ever bestow on him.

At the moment he needed to put in a few hours at the office and write up a report about the law enforcement meeting in Homer before heading off to his mother's house to pick up Addie. He grinned as he imagined her sweet little face lighting up as they were reunited. As he got in his truck and started the engine, he pushed all thoughts out of his mind of the attractive visitor to Owl Creek.

Sheriff Hank Crawford wasn't just a piece of Alaskan eye candy, she realized. He was a sweet-natured gentleman who happened to be close friends with Connor North. Between his gold badge and his relationship with the North family, he was causing warning sirens to clang in her head.

Sage didn't want to admit it, but she felt a little forlorn as she watched Hank head off toward the parking lot adjacent to the pier. She saw him climb into a hunter green truck before he roared off into the distance. Suddenly it hit her that she didn't know a single person in Owl Creek except the good-looking sheriff. She bit her lip. Perhaps her decision to come to Alaska had been based on emotion and grief over her mother's death rather than being a pragmatic decision to seek out her truths.

Had she made a mistake in traveling so far outside her comfort zone?

*The truth shall make you free.* The Bible verse from John washed over her. Lately it had really resonated with her. Truth was important. Being here in Owl Creek meant she was one step closer to uncovering the secrets from her past.

She shifted from one foot to the other, trying to keep her toes warm in her flimsy boots. Hank had been spot-on in his assessment of her winter gear. She made a

ere was a part of her that wondered if Nate and Willa
uld take one look at her and recognize her as their
n. Was such a thing even possible, or was she sim-
being fanciful? Maybe this was all a grand mistake.
haps she wasn't Lily North after all.

Piper slowed the van down and turned down a
w-covered lane lined with stunning spruce trees.
the end of the street stood a pewter-and-black sign
ouncing Miss Trudy's Bed and Breakfast. Piper
ed into a driveway and announced, "We're here!"
The inn was a beautiful yellow Victorian house with
te shutters. A bright blue door and a wraparound
ch lent the home an inviting look. With the snow
led on the roof, the bed-and-breakfast looked like
ething from a quaint Alaskan postcard. To complete
icture, a wooden statue of a moose sat knee-deep in
v in the front yard, and a Siberian husky ran toward
an, barking enthusiastically and wagging its tail.
age got out of the vehicle just in time to witness
dog jumping up on Piper and enveloping her in
ar hug. The petite young woman threw back her
 and laughed. "Okay, down, Astro. You almost
ked me over."

stro ran over toward Sage and began curiously
ing her. She held out her hand, obliging the husky.
n the dog began to lick her hand, Sage knew she'd
n a stamp of approval. Rather than follow them
ward the house, Astro ran toward the back of the
rty as if he was on the hunt for something.

 soon as they stepped inside the bed-and-breakfast,
 felt a heartwarming vibe pulsing in the air. The
lt cozy and warm. A blazing fire roared in the

mental note to purchase a sturdier pair, ones with in-
sulation from the snow and ice.

Miss Trudy Miller, the owner of the bed-and-breakfast
where she would be staying, had sent Sage a message
stating she would be picked up at the pier by her daughter Piper. Sage glanced at her watch, wondering if they
had gotten the pickup time wrong. Suddenly, a large
white van came barreling into the lot, stopping with a
loud squeal. A few seconds later, a woman came running toward her holding a sheet of poster board with
her name on it. Sage grinned at the sign being held up
by the petite woman with dark curly hair and tawny-
colored skin. She was wearing a red-and-black-checkered
jacket with a thick turtleneck peeking out from under-
neath it, along with a sturdy pair of boots.

"Are you Sage Duncan?" the woman asked breath-
lessly as she reached her side.

"Yes," she answered with a nod.

"I'm Piper. Trudy's daughter," she said, showcasing
a set of pearly whites as she smiled at her. "So sorry
I'm late. My van didn't want to start for me. Betsy
gets finicky once the temperature plummets. Let me
get your luggage."

"Oh no, I can manage. It's rather heavy," Sage explained, feeling guilty about making Piper carry her
supersized valise.

"No worries. I'm mightier than I look," the other
woman said with a wink, grabbing the bag and lug-
ging it toward her van. She looked over her shoulder
at Sage. "I grew up with an older brother who loved to
wrestle. It made me strong."

Sage chuckled at the image of Piper wrestling her

brother. She'd always wanted siblings but had been raised as an only child. Now that she looked back on it, she viewed it in a whole new light. She'd always known she was adopted. According to her father, Jane had struggled with infertility. Aunt Cathy, her mother's sister, had made a reference at her mother's funeral about desperate choices she'd made in the past. Although Sage had tried to get her to elaborate, her aunt refused to tell her anything further on the subject.

Sage reached for the poster-board sign, then picked up her small checkered duffel bag and followed behind Piper. She looked around her at the pine trees and the huge mountains looming in the distance. Wow. She really was in a completely different world right now, miles and miles away from sandy beaches and orange groves.

As they drove along snow-covered roads, Piper took the time to point out local landmarks, the shops in the charming downtown area and the Snowy Owl Diner where Piper worked when she wasn't helping out at the bed-and-breakfast. Sage sat back and tried to let it all soak in.

"Owl Creek isn't a very big town, but the folks here are tight-knit and friendly." She let out a throaty chuckle. "That's not to say there isn't the occasional drama breaking out, but it usually involves game night or the annual Alaskan cook-off competition. For the most part, this town is the very definition of serenity."

Sage could use a little peace right about now. She was trying to mourn her mother's death while wrapping her head around her unforgivable act. It was all

so hard to process. But she knew coming to
might give her the closure she so desperat

Piper continued. "If you want a good bi
come on over and check the diner out. We
a mean salmon chowder." Pride rang out i

"Mmm. Those both sound delicious," S
tite kicked up at the mere mention of food
eaten a bite since her layover in Seattle and
was beginning to grumble.

Sage's heart began to hammer inside
Piper pointed out a white chalet-style s
wanted sign hung in the window. "There'
North Star Chocolate Shop," Piper told
down as they drove past it. "It's one of the
tries of Owl Creek. There's a factory d
where they make the chocolate. They gi
a week." She licked her lips. "And they
olate samples."

"That sounds fun," Sage said. "I'll n
swing by there." She hoped her nerves
ing, but it was hard to stay calm, cool
when anything related to the North fa
tioned. She had researched the family
their names and faces. Nate and Willa
ents. They had two adult children, Con
Beulah North was the matriarch and h
olate company. She was married to
were also some other cousins, aunts
tant relations.

While looking at photos of the f
tried to find a resemblance betwee
Norths, but there really wasn't any

fireplace, colorful throws and pillows graced the living room area and picturesque photos hung on the walls.

"Hey, Mom. We're here," Piper called out, depositing Sage's luggage by the staircase.

"I'm in the kitchen," a voice called out.

Piper motioned for Sage to follow her as she walked down the hallway toward the sound of her mother's voice. Sage let out a low groan at the delicious smells wafting in the air. She wasn't sure what was cooking—perhaps pasta or bread—but it made her stomach lurch with hunger.

Once they crossed the threshold into the kitchen, Trudy greeted her.

"Sage! I'm so glad you've arrived safe and sound." The innkeeper was nothing like Sage had imagined. In her mind, Sage had envisioned Trudy as a sweet little old lady with white hair and granny glasses. But with her long wavy red hair, colorful bandanna and eclectic attire, she looked fun and stylish. Her green eyes were bright and engaging. Sage thought she was a stunning woman.

Before she could say a word, Trudy enveloped her in a tight hug. Without warning, Sage felt tears pooling in her eyes. This hug felt like home. It reminded her of her own mother and hundreds of embraces they had shared through the years. Trudy smelled like lemons and vanilla and kindness. She inhaled a deep breath and tried to compose herself.

When Trudy released her she stood face-to-face with Sage and looked deeply into her eyes. "You've had a long journey to get here. Why don't you let me show you to your room so you can rest up before dinner?"

"Thanks, Trudy, but if I lie down I probably won't come back down till morning," Sage said, chuckling.

"I have to head over to the diner to get ready for the dinner crowd, but I'll bring Sage's luggage upstairs to her room," Piper offered, leaning in to give her mother a kiss on the cheek. "Let's catch up later." She swung her gaze toward Sage. "It was great meeting you. Come on over to the diner soon. Your first meal is on me."

"Thanks for everything, Piper." Sage liked her a lot already. She appeared to be independent and feisty. And she had treated Sage like an old friend.

A few minutes later a loud bang rang out as Piper slammed the door behind her. Trudy winced, then muttered under her breath. "How many times have I told her not to slam the door?" She cocked her ear to the side, then let out a sigh that sounded like relief. Seconds later, a loud wailing sound echoed from down the hall.

"Now she's done it! She's woken up my grandbaby," Trudy said with a scowl.

Trudy scurried out of the kitchen, only to return a few moments later with a baby in her arms. She was rocking the little girl back and forth while making soft cooing noises to settle her. The baby calmed down and began to nibble on her fingers.

"Would you mind holding her for a moment?" Trudy asked Sage, holding the baby out to her before she even had a chance to answer. "I have to run upstairs to check on a radiator I just heard rattling."

"Sure," she answered, gently taking the baby in her arms. Although she didn't know a whole lot about kids, this little girl looked like a doll come to life. With her wide green eyes, bow-shaped lips and wispy curls, she was destined to be a heartbreaker.

"Hey there," Sage crooned. "Aren't you the sweetest little thing?"

The baby gazed up at her with a look of surprise etched on her cherubic face. Her lips began to tremble, and her eyes began to moisten.

"Oh no. Please don't cry," Sage pleaded. She began to hum and move from side to side in the hopes of soothing the little girl. What did people do to get babies not to fuss? The tyke opened her mouth and let out a wail.

Sage heard the opening and closing of a door, followed by heavy footsteps.

*Please, Lord. Let it be Trudy coming back to rescue me. I can handle second graders, but crying babies are a little bit out of my league.*

Suddenly, Hank appeared in the doorway with an expression of utter shock on his face.

His brows knit together in a frown. "Sage! What are you doing here? And why is my daughter crying loud enough to pierce an eardrum?"

# Chapter Two

Seeing Sage standing in his mother's house cradling his baby girl in her arms was a disorienting experience for Hank. On one hand it was incredibly heartwarming, but hearing Addie's earsplitting cries was also an agonizing sensation. He still hadn't gotten used to those wailing noises. It always made him feel as if he needed to protect his daughter against anything and everything that might harm her. As her sole living parent, Hank was all she had in this world, along with her grandmother and Piper.

"Hank!" Sage's eyes went wide. She looked at him then down at Addie then back at him again. "She's *yours*?" she asked.

"Dada!" Addie squealed, squirming in Sage's arms to get to him.

Hank moved toward his daughter with outstretched arms. He plucked Addie from Sage's grasp and began to rub her back and speak soothingly to her. It had taken him a while to get the hang of it, but now he knew how to placate his daughter. It was all in the tone and touch. Addie immediately began to calm down. She stuck her thumb in her mouth and began to vigorously suck it. Sage was still staring at him with her mouth hanging wide-open.

"She's mine all right. Every precious inch of her." He pressed a kiss against Addie's temple. "I assume you're staying here at the inn."

"Yes," she said with a nod. Her expression radiated confusion. "Trudy's your mother?"

He grinned at her. "So they tell me."

Sage didn't crack a smile. She still looked a bit shell-shocked.

Trudy came rushing back into the room. "Sorry to leave you hanging, Sage. False alarm." As soon as she spotted her son, the older woman's face lit up. "Hank! You're home. How was your trip?" She leaned up and planted a kiss on his cheek. "We missed you."

"It was time well spent," the sheriff said, putting his free arm around his mother. "But I'm happy to be back in Owl Creek. I missed my best girls something fierce."

"So you met Sage?" Trudy asked. "She's going to be staying here while she's visiting Owl Creek."

"We met," Hank said. "She was bonding with Addie when I got here."

Sage shot him a look of surprise. He wanted to laugh out loud. She probably thought holding a squalling baby was the furthest thing from bonding. It was fun to ruffle her feathers a tad. She seemed as if she had a tight rein on her emotions, and it would be nice to see her unwind a bit and let loose.

"How about sticking around for dinner?" Trudy

asked. "I'm making chicken piccata, one of your favorites."

Hank had smelled the meal cooking from the moment he'd walked into the house. Between the delectable aroma of the food and Sage's presence, he really wanted to stay for dinner. Originally he had planned to head back to his house so he could give Addie a bath and spend some quality time with her before supper, but all that flew out the window with his mother's invitation.

"Don't mind if I do," he said, making a funny face so Addie would giggle. He loved the sound of her tinkling laughter. It made him feel as if all was right with the world, even when it wasn't.

Sage smiled as she watched his interaction with Addie. It made her look even prettier, which didn't seem humanly possible. He didn't want to feel anything romantic for Sage, but there was something hovering in the air between them. A type of chemistry he couldn't ignore. And even though he was loath to pursue anything with her, it didn't mean he couldn't sit down for a meal at his mother's table and enjoy her company.

"How can I say no to my favorite dish?" he asked. "Why don't you let me set the table for you? How many of us are there this evening?"

"Just the three of us. Piper's at the diner. And those two journalists went in to town to eat," Trudy explained with a roll of her eyes. She heaved a little sigh. "Things have been so slow lately with reservations that I was hardly in a position to turn away those muckrakers. But I wish I could have. I just feel so guilty about giving them room and board when they're working overtime to stir up painful memories here in Owl Creek."

He reached out and patted his mother on the back. "You're just giving them a place to lay their heads, Mama. You're not responsible for what they write or the wounds they might be reopening."

"Muckrakers?" Sage asked with a frown.

Hank turned toward her. "Hordes of so-called journalists have descended upon us due to the anniversary of the kidnapping. They've been a bit intrusive. They're not all reputable outlets either. It's put a big strain on the town, mostly on the North family."

"Oh, that's terrible," Sage said, her features creasing with concern. "I can't imagine how painful it must be to have it all stirred up again."

Trudy made a tutting sound. "It was such an awful time. All of the memories of it have come crashing back even though most of us have tried to forget. It cast a pall over the whole town. There was a lot of suspicion and finger-pointing." She shivered. "No one wants to relive it."

"Willa and Nate pray every day to be reunited with Lily," Hank added gruffly. "Lord willing, it'll happen."

"They're always in my prayers," Trudy said. "I truly believe the Lord will show Lily the way back home."

Hank deposited Addie in her high chair and made quick work of setting the kitchen table. Trudy brought food over from the stove and began placing it on the plates. A nice salad and sourdough bread complemented the meal.

When they sat down to eat, they held hands while his mom prayed over the food. Hank couldn't deny how nice it felt to feel the warmth of Sage's hand in his. It had been a long time since he'd held a woman's hand in his own.

At one point during dinner, he looked over at Sage only to find her staring at his ring finger. He couldn't really blame her since he had done the same thing to her on the ferry. Nevertheless, Hank felt a sliver of annoyance as it dawned on him why she might be curious. Was Sage one of those people who judged single parents? He had dealt with a few over the past eight months and it made him feel defensive. A sudden noise from Addie caused him to turn in her direction. She was sitting in her high chair with her lip stuck out and a disgruntled expression stamped on her cute little face. It looked as if she was about to wail something fierce. Instinctively, he reached over to try to soothe her.

"Leave her be, Hank," Trudy said in a scolding tone. "You can't spoil her at every turn. You can't let her know she's got you wrapped around her little finger."

He let out a sigh, knowing his mother was right.

"I'm a single dad," he explained, locking gazes with Sage. "Addie's mom died in an accident about eight months ago. She was three months old at the time and had been living in Kodiak with her mother, Theresa. Sad to say, but I didn't even know she existed. Then in one fell swoop I found out I was her sole parent."

Sage let out a gasp. "Finding out about Addie must have turned your world upside down."

"It did," Hank acknowledged. "What I knew at the time about babies was next to nothing. But with the help of my mother and sister, I learned the ropes fairly quickly and day by day, things got better. Especially after I let God into my life and became a Christian." He sighed. "I loved Addie from the first moment I clapped eyes on her, but I think it took her a few weeks to reciprocate those feelings. She missed Theresa something awful. The first time she called me Dada I thought I might fly to the moon out of sheer joy."

"I can only imagine," she returned softly.

He met Sage's gaze head-on. "Sometimes there are things in life you never even knew you desperately needed to make you whole. Addie's one of those things. God is another."

Although Hank regretted being intimate with Theresa, his relationship with the Lord had been nonexistent at the time. He hadn't been a Christian. He had been reeling from the death of his stepfather and questioning everything in his life, which had led him to make poor choices. In the end, Addie had been an absolute blessing.

Trudy reached over and patted Hank's hand. "Addie couldn't ask for a finer daddy. Or a better man."

"Fathers and daughters have a very special bond," Sage agreed. "There's nothing quite like it in this world." She put a piece of chicken in her mouth and delicately chewed it before swallowing.

"It sounds like you're close to yours," Hank responded, immediately noticing the way Sage seemed to be fighting back tears. Clearly the subject of fathers and daughters had struck a nerve.

She nodded and looked down at her plate. "I've always been a daddy's girl. When I was growing up I seriously thought he hung the moon and that he was responsible for the stars twinkling up in the heavens."

Hank let out a low whistle as he laid his fork on his

plate. "I can only hope Addie feels that way about me someday. He must be a very loving father."

"He is," Sage murmured, toying with her food and not making eye contact.

Hank had the feeling she might be a little homesick. Perhaps she was having regrets about traveling all this way to Owl Creek. He had never been to Florida, but he knew it was a far cry from Alaska both in climate and the way of life.

He had a strange feeling about the mysterious newcomer. Perhaps it was his law enforcement background or maybe it was his desire to keep Sage at arm's length, but for the life of him, Hank couldn't rid himself of the notion that something was a bit off with Sage Duncan. Why had this beautiful woman come all the way to Alaska to a small hamlet like Owl Creek? And why did it seem as if she might be hiding something?

Shortly after dinner, Trudy brought Sage upstairs so she could settle in for the night. Sage let out a contented sigh as she entered the spacious room. It was beautifully decorated. The first thing she noticed was a queen-size mahogany sleigh bed with a pink-and-white-floral coverlet. Next to the bed sat a night table with a big bouquet of flowers. The wallpaper was old-fashioned—white swans against a gray background. It would be a lovely place to call home for the duration of her stay in town.

Trudy bid her good-night and advised her to sleep in tomorrow. Sage felt grateful for the innkeeper's nurturing manner and her desire to make sure she wasn't overtaxing herself. Truthfully, she was beyond exhausted, and it was fairly shocking she could still keep her eyes open.

Sage quickly went into the adjoining bathroom, washing her face and brushing her teeth in record time. Then she pulled on a pair of flannel pajamas and crawled under the covers.

However, as tired as she felt, her mind refused to shut down. There were so many thoughts whizzing through her brain. Hearing about the suffering of the North family hadn't been pleasant. She felt incredibly guilty that they were still on edge wondering what had happened to their daughter. Time had done nothing to close those wounds, and it angered her that people in search of a juicy story were making their suffering even worse.

Guilt pierced her insides. Could she single-handedly take away their pain? But what if she was wrong? All she had were her mother's dying words and a few newspaper clippings she'd found hiding in an old trunk. When she'd pressed him, her father had expressed astonishment about the kidnapping. According to him, he'd been completely in the dark. And the fact was, Jane hadn't been the most stable person. Sage had fuzzy memories of her mother having a breakdown when she was roughly eight years old. Could she have become fixated on the case and created this fantastical story?

Perhaps it was nothing more than a delusion. If she came forward and mistakenly made a claim about being Lily North, she would be no better than all the others who made false claims and subjected the North family to more agony.

No. It was far better for her to investigate the situation a little further and make peace with what had transpired. If that was even *possible*.

Hank's face flashed before her eyes. Just seeing him doting on his adorable baby girl had caused a hitch in her heart. Addie was pure sweetness and light; Hank's adoration for his daughter was unmistakable.

There was something so uplifting about seeing a man single-handedly raising his daughter. It reminded her of her own father and their incredibly close bond. At times during her childhood, Sage had felt as if she only had one parent due to her mother's illness. Her dad had always been there for her during the rough times, cheering her on and providing her with guidance. Sage had loved her mother dearly, but they hadn't shared the same powerful connection as she and her father.

Hank had asked her earlier this evening about her father. It had caused an immediate emotional response. For all intents and purposes, Eric Duncan was Sage's sole familial connection. He was all she had in the world. There had never been uncles or cousins or grandparents. As far back as she could remember, it had just been the three of them, along with Aunt Cathy, her mother's sister. Although Aunt Cathy hadn't been a big part of Sage's life, she'd been very close to her sister.

Sadly, she now knew that she wasn't the legally adopted child of Jane and Eric Duncan. Her whole life had been a huge lie. Sage didn't really know who she was. And while she should be mourning her mother's passing, all she could do was wonder if she had ever truly known the woman who'd raised her. Although her father had always been a man of faith, who regularly quoted scripture to Sage, took her to church services and volunteered for their church's outreach programs, her mother hadn't shown herself to be religious in any way, shape or form. Because of her mother's oddities, Sage hadn't ever questioned it. Perhaps it had been guilt, she reckoned, for having ripped a baby away from her parents.

Her father had been little or no help when she had questioned him about her mother's shocking confession. He had claimed Jane had told him she'd rescued her from two underage teens who hadn't been able or willing to raise her. He'd been convinced she had been an abandoned baby. Eric hadn't pressed for details since Jane had shown signs of mental instability and he'd never wanted to rock the boat. He had been so overjoyed to have a child in their lives after years of infertility that he had overlooked all the red flags and accepted her story without question.

All the color had been leeched from his face when Sage had shown him the newspaper clippings and the online reports regarding the kidnapping.

"I'm going to jail," he had said in a hoarse voice. "No one will ever believe I didn't play a role in taking you from your birth family."

"I won't let that happen, Daddy. Not ever," Sage had assured him. She had thrown her arms around him and held on for dear life, knowing she could never sacrifice the man who'd raised her. Never in a million years could she ever believe he had been her mother's accomplice in stealing a baby.

She would keep her promise to her father, no matter how dearly it cost her.

As Sage began to drift off to sleep, she murmured a prayer. God had been by her side throughout her life, and even though she was dealing with extremely difficult circumstances, she knew He wouldn't forsake her. Surely something good would come from her being in Owl Creek.

*Please, Lord, help me find the closure I'm seeking. Give me the strength to forgive my mother for her actions and to do what's right. I don't know what to do with all of these feelings or how to react when I come face-to-face with the North family. Grant me the wisdom to know how to proceed in the best interests of everyone involved.*

## Chapter Three

Hank drove down Main Street as a feeling of contentment spread through him. Snow had fallen late last night, covering the landscape with a healthy dusting of the frosty white stuff. There was no finer place in his opinion than Owl Creek, the place he was fortunate enough to call home. Being in Homer had been an interesting change of pace, but he wouldn't trade his hometown for anything in this world. He beeped his horn a few times at passersby, who called out friendly greetings to him in return.

He loved being out and about during office hours. He had just come from Opal Reed's house after rescuing her cat from the clutches of a snowy owl who had been hiding in her barn.

Opal had insisted on thanking him with tea and chocolate chip cookies. Earlier this morning he had been called out to settle a dispute between two fishermen who were feuding over a rare blue-colored king crab. Hank had managed to calm the situation down and convince Lou Baskin and Denny Phillips to share the unusual crustacean. When he'd left them the pair had been taking selfies together with the crab and cracking jokes about alerting the media. He chuckled at how raging controversies could be settled so amicably once people used their hearts and common sense.

Small-town life might not be for everyone, but he wouldn't trade it any day of the week for a high-paying job in a big city.

He frowned as he spotted a few journalists standing outside the North Star Chocolate Factory. They were like buzzards who had descended upon them in droves.

It was a downright shame how people had no respect for boundaries anymore. Nor did they understand that the North family had been through the worst tragedy a family could endure. In every practical way, they were still stuck in limbo with no sense of closure. He truly wondered if they would ever achieve it. Connor didn't talk about it a lot, but he knew the weight of it hung around his neck like an anchor.

Hank pulled into a spot right in front of the Snowy Owl Diner. The sheriff's office was only a short walk down the street from his go-to restaurant, which made it convenient. Once he stepped out of his squad car, he beat a fast path toward the diner. He was right on time for his weekly lunch with his two best buddies. His stomach groaned as he entered the establishment.

With a wave at Piper, who was behind the counter serving up meals, he headed toward a table in the back of the diner. Both Gabriel and Connor were already seated and engaged in an animated conversation. Hank slid into the booth next to Gabriel in a seat facing the door. As a sheriff he always wanted to be able to see who was coming and going. It had been ingrained in him when he was in the police academy.

"Hey, Sheriff. What's going on? How was Homer?" Gabe asked, clapping him on the back as a form of greeting. With his warm brown skin, dimples and soulful brown eyes, he exuded raw charm and personality. Hank couldn't remember a time when they hadn't been friends. Matter of fact, the three of them had been tight since they were in preschool. The three musketeers. One for all and all for one.

"It was great to connect with other law enforcement officials. I was able to spend some time with my buddy Boone Prescott, but I couldn't wait to get home to Addie," he confessed. He felt a little sheepish admitting it. Neither Connor nor Gabriel had even the slightest idea of how a child could transform a person's life. Until recently, he hadn't either. It wasn't all unicorns and sunshine, but it was the purest love he'd ever known. Hank hoped one day they would both know that type of unconditional love.

Connor shook his head and chuckled. "If someone had told me a year ago that you'd be hightailing it home to change diapers I would have laughed myself silly."

"Go ahead and laugh," Hank responded. "That little princess makes me happy just by looking in my direction."

"We know she does," Gabe chimed in. "No one deserves happiness more than you, buddy."

"Right back atcha," Hank responded.

Hank saw a glint of sadness flickering in Gabriel's eyes. Within seconds it vanished, replaced by his congenial smile. Hank felt a burst of sympathy for his friend. If things hadn't unraveled with Rachel, he might have had his own child by now. Instead, Gabe was still nursing a broken heart.

Connor sent Hank a look laced with meaning. He also understood Gabriel hadn't yet moved past having his bride run out on him forty-eight hours before the wedding. It hurt Hank to even think about how devastated his pal had been to lose the other half of his heart three years ago.

Rosie the waitress stopped by the table and poured coffee into Hank's mug. When he opened his mouth to put his order in, she shook her head. "They already ordered for you."

He looked at Gabriel and Connor, then shook his head. "How did you know what I wanted to eat?"

Rosie rolled her eyes. "Hank, you order the same thing every time you eat lunch here. Trust me, it's not a national secret."

As Rosie walked away, both Connor and Gabe threw back their heads in laughter. Hank joined in and began chuckling right along with them. Hanging out with these guys always made him feel better.

Both men were sought-after bachelors in Owl Creek. Connor, as the heir to the North Star Chocolate Company, was viewed as the ultimate catch, while most of the single ladies in town wanted to soothe Gabriel's shattered heart. Neither seemed particularly interested in settling down, however. Not that he should talk. Although he had once dreamed of picket fences and the storybook happy ending, he hadn't thought of those things in a very long time.

"So how are you holding up?" Hank asked Connor.

He could see the telltale signs of stress on Connor's face. Slight shadows rested under his eyes and creases lined the sides of his mouth. Hank knew he had a lot weighing on his mind.

Connor shrugged. "It's been rough, particularly on my folks. No wonder Braden headed off to parts unknown. The anniversary is always intense, but this year it's ten times worse with all the hoopla surrounding it."

Connor's younger brother, Braden, hadn't stuck around Owl Creek to endure the onslaught. He was off somewhere trekking in the Himalayas and seeking out adventures. Hank felt a surge of anger toward Braden for deserting his family during their hour of need. But he knew it wasn't right to judge the situation since he hadn't walked in his shoes. Being a sibling to a kidnapped and missing baby hadn't been easy on either Connor or Braden. The ripples of the kidnapping were far-reaching and complex.

Hank sat up straight in his booth when Sage walked into the diner. He watched as Piper came from behind the counter and greeted her with a big hug. It would have been impossible not to notice Sage in her hot-pink coat and matching beret. The sight of her gave Hank a little boost on an otherwise humdrum day. He felt his mood soaring.

He couldn't help but notice a few other men in the diner looking in her direction too. A feeling of possessiveness rose up inside him. An attractive woman showing up in Owl Creek was rarer than a comet sighting. It made him feel a little grumpy to know other guys might be interested in Sage, which was ridiculous since he wasn't in the market for romance…

"Hank? Hank? Earth to Hank!" Connor said, waving a hand in front of his face.

"Sorry. I got distracted," he muttered, managing to drag his gaze away from Sage.

"I see who has your attention and she's quite the looker," Gabriel drawled, his eyes alight with merriment. "I don't blame you one bit."

Connor turned around and craned his neck. Hank kicked him under the table.

"Ouch! What did you do that for?" Connor asked as he reached down and rubbed his shin.

"Because I don't want Sage to think we're staring at her," Hank grumbled.

"Even though we are," Gabe said with a good-natured chuckle.

"Sage? Who is Sage?" Connor asked, glaring at Hank.

"She's just arrived in Owl Creek from Florida and she's staying at my mom's inn," Hank explained. He didn't bother talking about how gorgeous she was or how she piqued his interest as no other woman had in quite some time.

"Please tell me she's not a journalist," Connor said with a groan, his expression mournful. "I'm a little sick of them shoving microphones in my face and taking my picture."

"Not even close," Hank answered. "She's a second grade teacher."

"Good!" Connor picked up his mug of coffee and took a long sip.

Hank swung his gaze up just in time to see Sage being seated at the booth diagonal to where they were sitting. She looked surprised when their eyes met. He lifted his mug up in greeting and waved to her with his other hand. She nodded in his direction and smiled.

Although Hank went back to his conversation with his best friends, he had a hard time focusing on chitchat when Sage was so close. She was proving to be a beautiful distraction, one Hank couldn't allow to disrupt his tranquil world.

From the moment she'd walked into the Snowy Owl Diner, Sage had felt as if she was on display. The stares and whispers of the townsfolk didn't escape her notice. She wasn't entirely certain if she was being treated with suspicion or mere curiosity. Was it possible they recognized something about her? Perhaps she was simply being paranoid. It was a bit awkward to walk around town harboring an explosive secret that could change the lives of several people in Owl Creek.

The diner was cheery and bright, with red leather booths and lemon yellow walls. The countertops were white marble and the floors were a black-and-white parquet. A five-foot bubble gum machine sat on display by the hostess stand.

As soon as she'd spotted her, Piper raced to her side, which had been a huge relief to Sage. The vivacious young woman had quickly whisked her over to a table and taken her order, reminding her that it was on the house. She felt thankful for Piper's presence. It felt a bit disorienting to know such a small number of people in town, and once again, she asked herself if coming here had been a colossal mistake.

"Don't worry about the stares," Piper said in a reassuring tone. "This is a small Alaskan town where everyone has known one another since the cradle. You're a novelty." Piper winked at her. "And a pretty one at that. You're going to get noticed."

*You're going to get noticed.* Her stomach sank upon hearing Piper's words. In actuality it was the last thing Sage wanted. Going under the radar had been her goal. She was beginning to realize it might be almost impossible in a town this size.

When Sage saw Hank seated a few feet away from her, there was no mistaking the little butterflies racing around in her stomach at the sight of him. Thankfully, the menu had provided a nice distraction from his close proximity, and she'd ordered herself a delectable lunch.

"Here's your bison burger with a side of rosemary fries," Piper announced as she placed Sage's plate down in front of her. "Take a bite and tell me if you like it."

Sage nodded and dug in. Piper was staring at her with barely contained excitement. Clearly, she wanted to know Sage's opinion about her culinary offerings.

The burger was juicy and cooked to perfection. The flavor of the meat popped on her tongue. It was definitely a unique taste she hadn't experienced before. "It's delicious," she said, feeling pleased she could give Piper positive feedback. "Cooked and seasoned to perfection."

"Yes!" Piper crowed in an animated voice as she raised her fist in the air. She did a little dance back toward the counter. Sage let out a giggle at her antics. Sometimes she wished she could be as spontaneous as the other woman seemed to be. Traveling to Owl Creek was probably the most daring thing she had ever done in her life. Only time would tell if it had been a wise decision.

Although she tried to block it out, Sage could hear the conversation between Hank and his two friends as clear as day. She knew without a doubt that one of his lunch companions was Connor North. He had walked by her table a few moments ago and she'd nearly let out a gasp of surprise at the sight of him. With his dark hair, blue eyes and striking features, he looked remarkably like the press photos of him. She felt her pulse quickening at the idea of being so close to someone who might be her blood relation.

"I've hired a team of private investigators to look into the case," Connor was saying, his tone radiating intensity.

"Do you really think they'll come up with anything after all this time?" their companion asked.

"I don't know, Gabriel. When it happened, my family hired the best private investigators money could buy, but the trail went cold," Connor responded. His expression looked grim. "I do know that I want this thing to be pursued until all leads are checked out. Someone has to know something. People just don't vanish into thin air."

"I completely agree with you," Hank said with a nod. "It would have been near impossible to pull off something like that without anyone knowing about it."

The man named Gabriel nodded and kept eating his meal.

Connor banged his fist on the table, causing both men to look up at him. "Someone needs to be prosecuted for abducting my sister! My family has been through the ringer and we deserve peace."

Suddenly their voices quieted, and they were now talking in hushed tones. A part of Sage felt relieved she could no longer hear their conversation. It had gotten way too intense.

*Peace.* Sage also wished peace for the North family. It was one of the reasons she had come to Owl Creek. She had hoped to discover that the North family was doing just fine all these years later. If that was the case, it would be much easier for her to walk away and stop torturing herself with images of faded press clippings and age-enhanced photos of a missing baby girl. She could put a lid on this whole nightmare.

But judging by Connor's anger and the things she had overheard him say, it wasn't even close to happening. The Norths were still struggling, and Connor was seeking vengeance. A reckoning of some sort for his sister's disappearance.

Sage shivered at the idea of what might happen if she revealed herself as Lily North. They might not even believe her story. And if they did, her beloved father could be the target of that quest for justice. He might be prosecuted and incarcerated. She might lose him forever.

Above all else, Sage couldn't allow that to happen. Throughout her life, especially when her mother had been having emotional difficulties, Eric Duncan had been her rock. Without him, she might not have made it through the tender middle school and teen years with her self-esteem and beliefs intact. He had taught her what it meant to be a child of God and a woman with strong convictions. Although she had loved her mother very much, her father had always been her world.

And that, she vowed, would never change.

By the time Hank had finished his lunch and calmed Connor down a bit, Sage was gone. He stuffed down his disappointment. He had intended to stop by her table on his way out and check in on her. But while he had been serving as a listening ear to Connor, Sage had slipped out of the restaurant. It shouldn't matter to him that she'd left, but it did. Hank really didn't want to examine the reasons why.

With a sigh, he headed out of the diner and walked down the street toward the sheriff's office. It wasn't as if he didn't have things to do. He had a bunch of paperwork to complete as well as checking in on a few older residents who lived farther out from town. Some of them didn't have working phones and tended to be off-the-grid. Hank made it his personal mission to make sure were safe and sound. Even if you were a born-and-bred Alaskan, winters could be challenging.

He hadn't walked more than twenty feet away from the diner when he saw a flash of pink. Sage was standing in the middle of the sidewalk looking around her in all directions.

A feeling of relief swept through him at the sight of her.

"Sage! You look a little confused. Are you lost?"

A sheepish expression crossed her face. "I got a little turned around. Trudy told me how to get to my destination, but needless to say, I walked in a big circle. I'm not sure where I went wrong."

"Where are you headed?"

"The chocolate factory. I was hoping to get a tour." She sniffed the air. "I'm surprised I can't smell it from here."

Hank grinned. "Oh, trust me. When you get close to it, you can smell the chocolate. It's utterly delectable."

Sage rubbed her mittened hands together like a little kid. "I'm looking forward to it. Chocolate is my weakness." It had been a long time since Hank had seen someone so excited about the North Star Chocolate Factory. Although the townsfolk loved it, they were also used to it, so people didn't tend to get overly animated about it. It was like having the Grand Canyon in your hometown. You knew it was spectacular, but you didn't rave about it all the time.

"How about I drive you over there? It's not far, but you're going to slip and slide all over the place in those boots." Hank really didn't want to keep harping on Sage's attire, but she was going to find out the hard way that frostbite was a very real thing in wintry Alaska.

Sage made a face and looked down at her suede boots. "Getting a sturdier pair is on my to-do list. Trudy told me to order some genuine, Alaskan-made boots. Lovely Boots she called them."

"That's good advice." He nodded, then pointed toward his squad car. "It's a quick ride to the chocolate factory. I don't mind taking you, Sage. That way you can orient yourself to the downtown area."

"I don't want to inconvenience you since you're on the clock," she demurred.

"No worries there," Hank said. "If there's any kind of emergency I can be reached at all times." He flashed her his best smile. "I consider it my civic duty since you're a visitor to Owl Creek."

"If it's not a bother, I accept," she acquiesced, walking beside him toward his squad car.

A feeling of triumph roared through him. There was something about this woman that made him want to be in her orbit. At the same time, he couldn't get rid of the sinking feeling she was being a bit standoffish. Or perhaps he was simply jaded based on his past. It wasn't fair to view her through a cracked lens.

He opened the door for Sage, then waited as she slid into the seat. Once he got behind the wheel, Hank started the engine and backed out of his spot and onto Main Street.

He looked over at her. "Have you ever gotten a ride in a squad car?"

"I can't say I have," she answered. "I've always been a rule follower. When I was a kid, I always colored inside the lines."

Hank wasn't sure whether Sage realized it or not, but her statement told him a lot about her. "I had my first ride in a squad car when I was six years old." Hank chuckled at the memory. "I stole a candy bar from the local market. Trudy insisted the store owner call the sheriff's office to report me. The sheriff arrived and put me in the back of the squad car and lectured me about how stealing was a crime and a sin. I had just learned the Ten Commandments so I was shaking in my boots."

"That's a bit harsh for a six-year-old," Sage said, making a tutting sound. "You must have been terrified."

"Not really." He cast her a glance. "You see, the sheriff was my father. And what I learned on that particular day has stuck with me ever since." Hank looked away from her and kept his eyes on the road. "On the way home he made a few stops to different townsfolk who needed his help. I don't think I'll ever forget the way they looked at him and how grateful they were for his assistance. On that very day I decided to be just like him so I could be the type of man he was."

"So you decided to become a sheriff like your dad. Have you managed to live up to his image?"

"Not even close," he said, letting out a ragged sigh. "But I'll keep trying."

As they rounded the block, Hank pointed out the side street he was cutting down from Main Street. "So from where you were standing in front of the post office, you head down Spruce Street, then make the left onto Forrest, then you continue straight and it'll be coming up on the left." A few moments later, Hank turned into the lot for the North Star Chocolate Factory. "And here we are," he announced. "The place where the chocolate goodness happens."

Sage was peering out the window with her face almost pressed against the glass. "What's going on here? Why is there such a large crowd? Perhaps they really are giving away free chocolate."

As he drove closer to the entrance, Hank noticed a swarm of journalists buzzing around the building. He recognized the two men who were staying at his mother's inn along with a host of others he'd seen around town over the last week. Releasing a groan, he parked his vehicle in front of the entrance. "Those are the muckrakers Trudy was talking about."

Sage looked at him with wide eyes. "Why are they all standing around?"

"I don't know, but I'm going to find out," he said, getting out of the squad car. Just for good measure, Hank flipped the blue-and-red flashing lights on. He prayed the situation didn't get ugly, but he needed to make sure order was maintained in his town.

By the time he went around to open Sage's door, she'd already stepped out of the squad car. She was looking at the mayhem as if she'd rather be anywhere else but here. He couldn't say he blamed her.

"These journalists are walking a fine line between freedom of the press and harassment," Hank muttered.

"Something tells me I won't be touring the chocolate factory today," Sage said, her expression radiating disappointment.

"Don't worry. I'll make sure you get a tour soon." Hank reassured her.

Suddenly Hank spotted Connor's parents, who were standing on the top step of the entrance to the factory. The journalists were at the bottom of the stairs, jockeying for position as they clicked their cameras and held out their microphones. Nate and Willa North had their arms joined and appeared to be preparing to make a statement. Nate held a piece of paper in his other hand.

Confusion swept over him. Connor hadn't mentioned anything about his parents having a press conference. Clearly he hadn't known anything about it.

Nate cleared his throat and effectively commanded everyone's attention. The crowd stilled and hushed. "Hello, everyone. Because the press is here in Owl Creek, we would like to do something we have con-

templated doing for twenty-five years." He reached
for his wife's hand. "We are humbly offering a sum of
one million dollars to anyone who can lead us to our
missing daughter, Lily, and to the person or persons
who abducted her."

Bedlam ensued with the journalists screaming questions at the couple until Nate raised his fingers to his
mouth and let out a deafening whistle. "Recent devel-
opments in the case have given us reassurance that
Lily is out there." He looked over at his wife who nodded at him.

Nate continued to speak. "We've received a letter
from the person who we believe stole our precious girl.
It states that Lily is alive and well. And it's given us our
best lead yet in finding our daughter and bringing her
abductors to justice. We're hoping a monetary offering
will be a huge incentive in aiding this investigation."

As town sheriff, Hank had known about the letter
for weeks now. He, along with the Norths' legal team
and the FBI, had encouraged the family to keep a lid
on it. Now the cat was out of the bag and the journalists
would have a field day with the information. He wasn't
sure what Nate and Willa were thinking in making the
information public, although he knew they were probably feeling desperate and running on fumes. Twenty-
five years was a long time to be in limbo.

Hank ran a hand through his hair and drew in a deep
breath. He turned to Sage to suggest she reschedule
her visit to the factory for another day, only to find
her gone. He whirled around and surveyed the crowd,
hoping to catch a glimpse of her hot-pink beret. Coming up empty, Hank walked over to his squad car just

to make sure Sage hadn't sought refuge inside the vehicle. The passenger seat was empty.

Sage had vanished into thin air without a single word of goodbye.

## Chapter Four

By the time Sage raced back to Main Street and away from the North Star Chocolate Factory, she felt out of breath and a bit light-headed. It had been a surreal feeling to find herself standing mere feet away from Nate and Willa North, the people she believed to be her biological parents. She had walked straight into a chaotic press conference and now her heart was full of so many conflicting emotions.

*Our precious girl.* Hearing those words had caused a tightening sensation to spread through her chest. Her feelings were all over the place after hearing the longing in Nate North's voice. It brought to the surface emotions she'd been stuffing down her entire life. There had always been a part of her that didn't feel as if she'd belonged. In truth, she hadn't. She had been living Sage Duncan's life when in reality she'd been Lily North the whole time.

At this rate she wasn't sure she could keep up this facade without blurting out the truth.

Was it cruel to keep silent when her birth parents were desperately searching for her? Her mind was scrambling to process what she'd just heard. Had her mother really sent the North family a letter? A confession? And, if so, was there a trail leading directly back to her father? Jane Duncan had always been unpredictable, and even though she'd been bedridden in the last few weeks of her life, Sage knew her mother had always been extremely resourceful.

Perhaps she should have stayed back at the chocolate factory to learn more, but her body had been in flight mode and her legs had carried her swiftly away from the press conference as if on autopilot.

Sage bit her lip. Before she went off the deep end, she needed facts. She wasn't going to fall apart until she had something concrete to go on. Perhaps the letter had been written by an attention seeker motivated by the twenty-fifth anniversary of the kidnapping. Hadn't Hank told her that scam artists had been coming out of the woodwork as of late? Maybe she was worrying about nothing.

Still, Sage felt a bit guilty about leaving Hank in the lurch since he'd been so kind to her. He probably thought she was a flake after she'd bailed on him. She let out a deeply held breath, watching as the cold air condensed in front of her eyes. Why was she even fretting about it? She didn't need a town sheriff in her business. It would be like putting her feet too close to the fire. Hank had strong ties to the North family and he worked in law enforcement. In this explosive situation, those were two strikes against him.

Too bad he was all kinds of handsome and a bit of a sweetheart. Driving her over to the chocolate factory had been a nice gesture, but she should have refused the offer. Sage couldn't allow herself to get too close to anyone in this town, particularly not a man who'd vowed to uphold the law.

A quick glance at her watch told her she still had a few hours before she was due to meet up with Trudy, who was giving her a ride back to the bed-and-breakfast. She'd been planning to spend the afternoon touring the chocolate factory, but the impromptu press conference had changed her plans. Perhaps she could kill some time exploring the shops on Main Street, although it would be mighty embarrassing if Hank drove by and spotted her. She didn't have a single idea as to how to explain why she'd run off.

Sage was standing a few feet away from a quaint shop window adorned with lovely curtains and a display of brightly colored teapots. She moved closer and pressed her face against the frosted-over window to get a better look. The interior looked cozy and warm. A soft glow emanated from inside. It seemed like the perfect place to take a load off her feet.

She looked up at the dainty gold sign hanging above the entrance. Tea Time. It was the shop Trudy had told her about this morning. Frankly, she could use a nice cup of tea at the moment. If she ducked inside she could avoid the possibility of running into Hank and having to explain why she'd taken off. What could she possibly say to explain her disappearing act?

Sage slowly pushed open the door and stepped inside. The scent of lavender hung in the air. She looked around with a feeling of wonder. It felt as if she had stepped back in time to another era. The tea shop was decorated with plush velvet chairs, stunning rugs and silk fans hanging on the walls. A brightly lit chandelier hung from the ceiling and brocade wallpaper graced the walls. A whimsical photo of a bear in a pink tutu hung by the front desk, along with an old-fashioned telephone.

The place was fairly empty but there was a low hum of voices emanating from the dining room. A tall woman with dark brown skin approached Sage with a welcoming smile. "Hello. I'm Iris Lawson. Welcome to Tea Time. Are you a party of one?" she asked.

Sage nodded. "Yes, it's just me today."

"Perfect. Let me show you to a table." Sage followed behind Iris, taking in all the lovely details of the establishment along the way.

Once she was seated at a table, Iris handed her a menu. "I'll be back in a few minutes to take your order. Let me know if you have any questions."

Sage looked around her with curiosity. There was an older woman sitting by herself at a neighboring table. She was a striking woman with jet-black hair streaked with silver. She had a widow's peak much like Sage's own and she was wearing an elaborate navy blue hat with a peacock feather on top. A pearl necklace graced her neck. She looked regal. Sage made eye contact with the woman and smiled.

"Are you a first timer?" the woman asked.

Sage nodded. "Yes. It looked so lovely when I peered through the window, I couldn't resist coming inside." Truthfully, it reminded her of a tearoom her mother used to take her to when she was a little girl of eight or nine. The sweet memory was jarring in the face of her mother's shocking confession. At the moment she was struggling to make sense of the dual sides of Jane Duncan. Loving mother versus heartless criminal.

The woman continued to speak. "Isn't it exquisite? I make it a point to come here several times a week. You're in for a treat."

Sage had a niggling feeling she'd seen this woman before. She looked so familiar.

Suddenly it came to her. She was Beulah North, the matriarch of the North family. Studying her birth family prior to her arrival in Owl Creek had been a smart move on her part. Strangely, it gave her comfort to recognize a few people from her family tree.

"I don't blame you," Sage murmured. "It's a beautiful place to sit back and relax."

"If you're not waiting for anyone, I'd love some company. It appears my date has stood me up." Beulah nodded toward one of the empty chairs at her table.

"I'd be happy to join you. Thanks for asking," Sage said as she gathered up her purse, then stood up and made her way over to Beulah's nearby table. Although Beulah had no way of knowing it, Sage was so nervous her knees were knocking together. She wanted so badly to make a good impression on her grandmother.

"I'm Beulah North. And you are?" she asked, sticking out her hand to Sage.

"Sage Duncan," she replied, shaking the elegant woman's hand.

"Nice to meet you, Sage. Are you a newcomer to Owl Creek? Surely I'd remember seeing a young lady as beautiful as you are around town."

Sage felt herself blushing. "You're too kind."

"Not really," Beulah said, wrinkling her nose. "I'm

known in Owl Creek for telling it like it is." She winked at Sage. "Some people here in town find it off-putting at times."

Sage chuckled. "To answer your question, I'm only a temporary resident here in town."

"Oh, is that so?"

"Yes. I'm visiting for roughly six weeks…and I'm a teacher, so I suppose you could call it a sabbatical."

Beulah regarded her with knowing eyes. "Say no more. I know what it's like to be overwhelmed and want to hide away from the world for a bit." She reached across the table and patted Sage's hand. "Owl Creek is the perfect place to reflect and take stock of your life."

Sage opened her mouth to tell Beulah she hadn't come to Alaska for those reasons. But what would she say? It was out of the question to blurt out her real reasons for making this incredible trek to Alaska. Beulah might pass out if she told her she was her long-lost stolen grandbaby. Or she might assume Sage was yet another fraud bent on deception. No, for the time being, it was far better for Beulah and the rest of the townsfolk to believe she'd come to Owl Creek seeking a refuge from the storms of life. Once the truth came out, her father could be swept up in a cloud of suspicion and legal wrangling. The thought of it made her shudder.

Iris provided a welcome distraction by appearing at their table with a wide grin on her face and pushing a tea cart laden with goodies. "I wondered if the two of you might wind up sitting together. Afternoon tea is much better with company." She looked over at Sage.

"I brought over Beulah's favorite lavender tea. Let me know if you'd like something else instead."

"I'm not fussy about tea or food, so I'm sure it will be fine," Sage said, inhaling the heady aromas of the various teas. "Everything smells delicious."

Iris placed the steaming teapot down on the table along with a three-tiered stand overflowing with finger sandwiches, tiny cakes, scones and miniature muffins. Even though she'd recently eaten lunch, Sage's hunger kicked in at the sight of the scrumptious treats.

"Enjoy!" Iris said before walking off toward another table.

Beulah lifted the teapot and leaned toward Sage to pour tea into her cup. Her movements were graceful. Once Beulah served herself, they both began adding sweeteners and milk to their cups. Sage reached for a cucumber sandwich and a blueberry scone. The two of them settled into a companionable silence as they drank their tea.

"Do you like chocolate?" Beulah asked. She seemed to be sitting on the edge of her seat, anxiously awaiting Sage's reply.

"Is that even a question?" Sage asked with a chuckle. "I didn't know it was possible for a person *not* to like chocolate." She lifted her teacup up to her mouth and took a sip of the piping hot tea.

Beulah threw her head back and let out a hearty laugh. Her tinkling laughter filled the air and warmed Sage's heart. Beulah North radiated an air of goodness. Given everything the North family had been put through, it made Sage feel hopeful. As awful as the kidnapping had been it clearly hadn't destroyed Beulah or her zest for life.

"I'm serious," she said. "I love all kinds. Milk chocolate, dark chocolate, white chocolate. Chocolate-covered cherries. Truffles. Pecan clusters. Caramel chocolate. Honestly, I'm crazy about all of them."

"I couldn't agree with you more. In my world, chocolate is a staple. I've loved it ever since I came out of the womb, which is one of the dozens of reasons I married my husband, Jennings, bless his heart. His family created the North Star Chocolate Company right here in Owl Creek."

"That's impressive. I've heard a lot about it. I really wanted to take a tour of the factory this afternoon, but it was quite hectic over there this morning with the press conference and the media crush."

Suddenly, there was a look of distress etched on the older woman's features. Sage could have kicked herself for blurting out the news. Perhaps Beulah hadn't known anything at all about her family's statement to the press. If that was true, Sage had spilled the beans.

"I'm so sorry," she said. "That was insensitive of me. I didn't mean to dredge up an uncomfortable topic."

Beulah paused to take a sip of her tea. "There's no need to apologize. I knew all about the press conference, which is why I'm sitting right here at this table sipping my favorite tea and enjoying your lovely company. I opted out of it."

Sage sensed Beulah wanted to talk, so she simply stayed quiet and listened.

"This time of year isn't easy for my family," Beulah admitted. "I'm sure you've heard a little something about it, but twenty-five years ago we suffered a terrible loss. My sweet granddaughter Lily was stolen from us." She shuddered. "Gone without a trace. It's amazing how in some ways time has stood still and we're all still waiting for some type of closure. I just couldn't go to that dark place today." Beulah scoffed. "I must sound like a real chicken, but my heart has been knocked around a bit in the years since we lost Lily. I don't want to hope for her return only to have my heart ripped out of my chest again. My sweet Jennings has been affected deeply by it. Most days he doesn't even venture outside."

Tears pooled in Beulah's eyes, which in turn caused a huge lump to rise to Sage's throat.

Instinctively, she reached across the table and squeezed Beulah's hand. "You don't sound like a chicken at all. You sound like a woman who has been through a terrible ordeal. I'm so sorry." It hurt to see Beulah so wounded and to know that she was tied up in the pain the North family had endured. It was one thing to know it from a distance, but now she was up close and personal to the living, breathing people whose lives had been forever altered by her mother's selfish actions.

"You're a very kind woman, Sage. And I'm going to personally make sure you receive that tour of the chocolate factory." She beamed at Sage. "Matter of fact, I'm going to show you around myself." Beulah's gaze drifted to a point past Sage's shoulder. Within seconds, Sage looked up to find Hank standing next to their table with his arms folded across his chest. His steely gaze was focused on Sage.

"Fancy meeting you here," Hank drawled, his eyes full of questions. "I was wondering where you'd disappeared to. Was it something I said?"

Hank couldn't deny the slight thrill he got from putting Sage on the spot. The look on her face when he'd appeared at her table had been priceless. Her eyes were as wide as saucers and her mouth had opened without any words coming out. He reckoned it was safe to say she was speechless. Beulah, on the other hand, seemed as if she had plenty to say to him.

"Oh, look what the cat dragged in. It's my gentleman companion." Beulah dramatically pulled up her sleeve and looked at her watch. "And he's only thirty-five minutes late."

He leaned down and pressed a kiss on Beulah's cheek. "Forgive me, Miss Beulah. I didn't forget about our tea date, but I've been putting out a few fires at the chocolate factory. There was a real commotion over there."

Beulah wrinkled her nose and made a harrumphing sound. "As I live and breathe! I was stood up for a press conference!"

Hank spread his arms wide. "Well, I'm here now, aren't I? Better late than never."

"You're incorrigible. I should warn all the women in Owl Creek about you," Beulah scolded.

"You know I only have eyes for you," Hank said in a teasing tone.

"If I was only twenty years younger," Beulah quipped, batting her eyelashes.

Hank wagged his finger at her. "Now who's being incorrigible?"

Iris appeared at their table and leaned in to give Hank a hug. "Why don't you sit down, and I'll bring another tea-and-saucer set over?"

"Thanks, Iris," Hank responded. He was still getting used to calling her by her first name after a lifetime of calling her Mrs. Lawson. Gabriel's mother was one of his favorite Owl Creek residents. She was a devoted mother with a strong entrepreneurial spirit.

"I don't want to intrude," he said, his gaze swinging toward Sage, who appeared slightly uncomfortable. Did he make her nervous? Or was she feeling awkward due to her disappearing act?

"Don't be silly!" Beulah patted the seat next to her. "Sit down, Hank, and join us. I take it the two of you already know each other." Her eyes twinkled as she looked back and forth between them. Hank let out a sigh. If Beulah was looking for any dirt about his relationship with Sage, she was bound to be sorely disappointed.

Sage nodded. "Hank and I met on the ferry over to Owl Creek. I'm staying at Trudy's inn while I'm here in town, so it was a pretty funny coincidence to run into each other there."

Hank wanted to laugh out loud at the look of disappointment stamped on Beulah's face. He would bet his last dollar she'd been imagining a deeper connection between him and Sage.

Why did women in this town always want to pair him up with someone? Perhaps he needed to walk around town with a sign announcing he was happily single and not looking for romantic entanglements. Instead of devoting himself to a woman, Hank had decided to give fatherhood 100 percent of his time and attention. He knew he'd never regret that particular decision.

Hank sank down into a seat and thanked Iris as she placed a teacup in front of him. If anyone had told him a few years ago that he would become a tea fanatic, he would have called them all kinds of crazy. But ever since Iris opened up the doors of Tea Time, his love of tea had risen dramatically. There wasn't a single thing he didn't like about teatime. The various flavors of tea. The dainty little cakes and sandwiches. Gabriel and Connor enjoyed giving him a hard time about it, but he didn't mind the ribbing.

Hank raised the cup to his mouth and let out a sound of appreciation. "Nothing hits the spot like lavender tea."

"It's delicious," Sage murmured. "The flavor is a bit unusual, but I'm enjoying it."

"It's fun to try new things, isn't it?" Beulah asked. "It's all part of your grand Alaskan adventure."

Sage grinned at Beulah and it made him feel a little bit off-kilter. Much as he hated to admit it, Sage Duncan drew him in like a moth to a flame. Her gentle beauty and the slight air of mystery hovering around her was extremely appealing. He didn't even want to look in her direction too much, for fear he might be staring. Hank dragged his gaze back to Beulah, knowing he was heading into dangerous territory every time he was in Sage's presence.

Beulah sent him a pointed look. "So, what did I miss, Hank? Over at the factory."

For a moment, Hank hesitated. He didn't know Sage well enough to discuss the issue in front of her, but after today's press conference the subject was out there for public consumption. It would soon be splashed all over the internet and the covers of newspapers.

He locked gazes with Beulah. Even though he knew she was a tough cookie, she looked a little frayed around the edges. The toll of the twenty-fifth anniversary of the kidnapping was clearly getting to her. "Willa and Nate let the media know about the letter they received. They're determined to offer a hefty monetary reward for any leads on Lily's whereabouts."

Beulah made a tutting sound. "If money had been the objective, wouldn't there have been a ransom demand all those years ago?"

"Honestly, I think they're hoping an accomplice or an informant might have some information and be motivated by the reward. It's a long shot, but the letter gave them hope."

"How do they know the letter is genuine?" Sage asked. "Are you able to disclose what the letter said?"

Hank looked over at her, marveling at her wide brown eyes flecked with gold. Her question about the authenticity of the letter was a good one, but once again, Hank found himself struggling to maintain an air of professionalism. As town sheriff, he knew certain things about the Lily North case that he couldn't reveal and it wouldn't be right to share that information with Sage. His own father had been sheriff at the time of the kidnapping. It had been Tug Crawford's dream to solve the case, although his premature death made it an impossibility.

Before Hank could respond, Beulah jumped in.

"It was an apology of sorts, I suppose. According to

the letter, Lily is alive and this individual raised her as her own child. The person who left the letter put some breadcrumbs in it," Beulah explained. "There was one major detail that was never reported after Lily was taken." The older woman's hand shook and she rested the teacup on the table. "When Lily was stolen, the kidnapper took her baby blanket along with her. It was an heirloom piece and very distinctive because it had an owl motif. My daughter-in-law Willa made it herself. It was referenced in the letter."

Hank frowned at Beulah. She shouldn't have disclosed those facts to Sage. There were so few people who had been privy to the details about the baby blanket. For all these years the circle had been incredibly small, and the media had never caught wind of it. Now that Beulah had let the cat out of the bag there was no telling who might pounce on the information.

"Beulah, I don't think it's a good idea to share specific details of the case." He hadn't meant to sound harsh, but he could tell by Beulah's and Sage's reactions that he'd sounded severe. Sage appeared to be mortified while a storm was brewing in Beulah's eyes.

"I'm sorry. I wasn't trying to pry," Sage said, her tone apologetic. Her cheeks were flushed, and she looked down at her teacup. Hank wanted to kick himself. She looked so humbled, as if she had been put in her place. He had only meant to warn Beulah against revealing so much to a virtual stranger.

Beulah abruptly stood up. "I won't be treated like a child, Hank Crawford! I may be from the older generation, but I still have my full faculties about me. After twenty-five years I have the right to discuss Lily's disappearance however I see fit." She stomped her foot. "This has been a terrible day, full of reminders of everything my family has lost. Twenty-five years later and I'm still expected to walk on eggshells. It's no wonder poor Jennings stays cooped up in the house and refuses to be a part of the world."

Hank's heart sank. He had never seen Beulah so upset. She was clearly unraveling, and it was all his fault. He had crossed a line by chiding her. Although his intentions were honorable, his delivery had been terrible.

"Beulah, forgive me," Hank said, his voice filled with remorse. "I'm so sorry for upsetting you."

Beulah ignored him and looked directly at Sage. "I'm sorry, my dear, to leave so abruptly, but it seems as if everything is catching up to me all at once. I'm feeling terribly tired at the moment and all I want to do is go home and lie down."

Sage reached out and enveloped Beulah in a tight embrace. As Hank watched, the two woman clung to each other for dear life. Sage was murmuring something to Beulah that he couldn't quite hear. When they pulled apart, Beulah had tears glistening in her eyes. "I'll be in touch about your tour of the chocolate factory," she told Sage, who nodded enthusiastically.

"Can I walk you to your car?" Hank asked, wincing at the fierce look Beulah shot him in response.

"I managed to get myself here. Surely I can see myself out," Beulah answered before walking away from the table with her head held high. Her body language radiated a fiery anger.

Hank shook his head. "Open mouth, insert foot,"

he muttered. He was disappointed at himself for sending Beulah into a downward spiral. She was his dear friend and his best friend's grandmother, not to mention the grand dame of Owl Creek. He should have understood how raw her nerves were regarding the topic of her missing granddaughter.

Hank looked over at Sage. "So, do you want to unload on me too? Go ahead, Sage. I can take it. Tell me what a colossal idiot I am."

## Chapter Five

Sage shook her head at Hank. She had only been in Owl Creek for a few days and somehow she'd landed smack-dab in the middle of a squabble between the town sheriff and her paternal grandmother. So much for keeping her head down and staying away from controversy. It felt like she was right in the thick of it.

Although she felt a great deal of sympathy for Beulah, she couldn't place the blame squarely on Hank. It was fairly obvious to her that Beulah had been sitting on an emotional powder keg. No doubt it had been years in the making. Sadly, it had all blown up due to the tremendous stress she was under and the pressure of the twenty-fifth anniversary of Lily's abduction.

"I don't think you're an idiot at all," Sage said. "I think Beulah is hurting and what you said rubbed her the wrong way. I can't imagine how painful it would be to go through an ordeal like the one the North family has endured."

Hank's expression was somber. "It's like a gaping hole that never gets filled. That's how Connor explained it to me once."

"Does he remember his sister?" Sage asked. She tried to keep her tone neutral, although she was eager to hear his response. Growing up as an only child, she had longed for siblings. It would have made the feelings of loneliness more bearable. Knowing she had two brothers was an amazing feeling, even though in all likelihood she would never connect with them in any meaningful way. She was still determined to protect her father at all costs and the only way to do so was to retain her anonymity.

Hank nodded. "Connor was five years old when Lily was taken. He has vivid memories of his baby sister. Matter of fact, Connor was the one who came up with her name. He still feels a deep connection to her."

Suddenly her throat felt as if it was clogged with cotton balls. "That's really sweet."

"I wouldn't describe Connor that way," Hank said with a throaty laugh. "He's a good guy, but he isn't always warm and fuzzy. I couldn't ask for a more loyal friend though." His voice softened. "I think the tragedy caused him to grow a hard outer shell. It's difficult for him to trust folks."

"That's understandable. He's grown up in the shadow of an inexplicable tragedy," she responded, her mind whirling at the ripple effect the kidnapping had set in motion. So many lives had been altered by her mother's heinous crime. She'd hurt so many people with her twisted actions. Ultimately, Jane Duncan had gone to the grave without having to make amends for all the harm she'd caused. Although she loved her mother, it still seemed very unfair to Sage.

The kidnapping explained so much about her mother's lack of faith. How could a person be a believer and justify stealing another woman's child? Had she repented on her deathbed? Had her mother found Jesus in her final days? Perhaps she had written the letter as a way to make amends and reassure the North family that Lily was still alive.

"Are you heading back to the inn?" Hank asked, pulling her out of her thoughts.

Sage glanced over at the clock on the wall. "Actually I have another hour to kill before Trudy picks me up. I really need to get a rental car so I can explore Owl Creek without bothering your mom. She's been so gracious, but I don't want to impose on her."

"I'm sure she doesn't mind, but I can quickly swing you over there if you like. It will give me an opportunity to pop in on Addie."

"That would be great if you can spare the time," Sage answered.

He dug into his pocket and pulled out a cell phone. "Sure thing. Let me call my mom and let her know." Sage waited while Hank made the phone call. It was nice to hear the sweet way he spoke to Trudy on the phone. They clearly shared a close, loving relationship. Although she had known her own mother loved her, their relationship had always been strained. Jane Duncan's mercurial moods had cast a pall over Sage's childhood, and she had never known from one moment to the next which way the wind would blow with regard to her mother's temperament.

Iris walked toward them and said in a hushed tone, "Beulah said to put everything on her tab right before she stormed out of here."

Hank grimaced. "As usual, Beulah is one step ahead of me. I was planning to pay today. She loves having the last word, doesn't she?"

"Don't take her mood personally, Hank. She's going through a tough time. The two of you have such a wonderful friendship. This is just a little bump in the road." She patted him on the arm. "She needs you more than ever now."

Hank's jaw tightened. "She can lean on me. I'll always have her back." Sage shivered at the intensity in the sheriff's voice. She pitied the person who tried to mess with Beulah.

"It was so nice to meet you, Sage," Iris said, clasping Sage's hand in her own.

"Likewise," she answered, feeling a bit more relaxed due to Iris's down-home hospitality. She and Beulah had made Sage feel as if she belonged in Owl Creek even though she was virtually a stranger to them. Most places didn't welcome folks like this, Sage realized. Perhaps there really was something special about this Alaskan town. She felt a sudden pang. What would it have been like to grow up in Owl Creek as a member of the North family? She imagined life would have led her down a completely different path.

Once Iris walked away, Hank turned toward her. "Ready to go?"

Sage nodded and followed behind him as he walked toward the exit. The place had filled up considerably while she was enjoying teatime. Hank was cordial to all of the guests as he passed by their tables, nodding and holding his hand up in greeting. Everyone clearly loved the sheriff. It was written all over their faces. Sage couldn't help but notice the curious stares in her direction. Like Piper had told her earlier, the towns-folk in Owl Creek had known one another all of their lives. She stuck out like a sore thumb in this small Alaskan hamlet.

Once they were outside, Hank walked ahead and opened the passenger door of his squad car for her. She slid into the seat and rubbed her hands together, praying the car would heat up quickly. After he set-tled himself behind the wheel, Hank began driving down snow-packed roads and riding past all of the brightly colored retail shops. Along the way he pointed out a pottery shop, a small thrift store and various landmarks. A marble statue of an owl sat in the town square.

"So, I have to admit I'm curious," Hank said, turn-ing toward her. "Why did you run off earlier? It was the fastest disappearing act I've ever seen in my life, and I keep law and order for a living."

Sage squirmed in her seat. She should have known it would only be a matter of time before he brought the subject up again. There was no way she could tell Hank the truth, but she didn't want to lie either. "Honestly, it was all a bit overwhelming to me," she admitted. "There was such a crush of people there. I felt like I couldn't breathe." There. She had managed to tell Hank the truth, even though she'd left out a few vital details.

He turned his gaze back toward the road. "It makes

sense, especially since you're in a new town where you don't really know a whole lot of people."

"I shouldn't have just taken off," she said, her tone apologetic. "I'm sorry about that. It wasn't very considerate of me."

"It's okay." Hank shot her an easy grin. "Things are a bit unusual here in Owl Creek these days. Normally it's much quieter, but there's nothing ordinary about all of this media attention and hoopla. Our small town has turned into a hot spot for news outlets. For a lot of folks, it's stirring up a lot of painful memories."

"I hope the Norths realize that by giving the press conference they're inviting even more media scrutiny into their lives. It might get worse before it gets better." Sage bit her lip. She felt guilty about withholding the truth from the North family. With a few words she could put them out of their misery. But, given the high stakes, it was out of the question.

"They were advised against staging the press conference, but they're desperate," Hank explained, shaking his head. "Twenty-five years is a long time to hold on to hope. I think this is their last-ditch effort to bring Lily home."

Sage had a funny, gnawing feeling in the pit of her stomach. Hank's words about bringing Lily home weighed heavily on her conscience.

She felt so conflicted. A part of her didn't want her birth family to give up on the idea of finding her, while another part of her wanted to make sure her father was safe from any legal fallout if the truth was discovered. For her entire life, Sage's father had been her protector and now she was returning the favor by keeping quiet about being Lily North. She couldn't live with herself if she betrayed her dad. Sage owed him her loyalty.

For a few moments she decided to focus on the snowy landscape outside the car window.

It felt very calming and provided a nice distraction from her chaotic thoughts. This land was so very different from Florida. Majestic trees covered with fluffy snow dotted the terrain. A yellow-and-black caribou-crossing sign drew her attention to the side of the road.

Caribou? Wasn't it a type of reindeer? She let out a low chuckle. She really was in a whole new world here in Owl Creek.

By the time they pulled up to the inn, Sage's head felt a bit clearer. She needed to keep reminding herself where her loyalties lay. She had been a Duncan for twenty-five years. Even if she wanted to tell the Norths about her mother's confession and put an end to their suffering, Sage had no idea where things would go from there. It wasn't as if she would suddenly become a member of this illustrious Alaskan family. In many ways it was too late to forge a connection. She would never truly fit in, no matter how they tried to embrace her as one of their own. And there would be so many questions about her mother and why she'd committed such a terrible act. How could Sage ever explain it when she was still grappling for answers herself?

"Thanks for the ride," Sage said as soon as the car stopped, taking off her seat belt and then reaching for the door handle. Hank didn't make a move to get out of the driver's seat. "Are you coming in?" she asked.

He ran a hand over his jaw. "You know what? I think

I'll just head back to the sheriff's office. I don't want to upset Addie by popping in and then leaving again."

"But she'll be so happy to see you." Earlier Hank had seemed so excited about dropping in to get a glimpse of his daughter, but now it appeared as if he'd talked himself out of it. She couldn't help but wonder why.

He shook his head. "I don't want to derail her routine. I've been reading some books about child-rearing and I'm trying my best to put her needs before mine. Going inside for a few minutes might be confusing to her."

Although she didn't know Hank all that well, Sage could see he was struggling not to jump out of the car and beat a fast path to Trudy's door. His love for Addie was evident every time he mentioned her name. It was plain to see she was wrapped around his heartstrings.

"It must be hard making those kinds of choices," Sage said. "As a single father, a lot rests on your shoulders, doesn't it?"

He let out a ragged sigh. "It's tricky sometimes, having to make all of the decisions myself. Honestly, I never imagined myself doing this all alone. And I know I'm so fortunate to have such a supportive mother and sister, but parenting is a tough job. Way more difficult than being town sheriff."

Sage impulsively reached out and grasped his right hand, which was tightly clenching the wheel. "First of all, I think you should just take a deep breath and make the most of the moment. I'm around little kids all the time. They value every second they spend with their parents. Think about it. In a blink of an eye she'll be in elementary school. You'll never get these precious minutes back. Cherish them."

Hank locked gazes with her and she watched as a smile eased its way onto his handsome face. "My dad used to say that to me all the time. Cherish the moments." He grinned. "I think about him each and every day, but somehow I'd almost forgotten that saying of his. Thanks, Sage, for reminding me."

"You're very welcome," she murmured. Trudy had told Sage about losing her husband when Hank was a small boy and then finding love a second time around with Piper's father. There had been such tenderness in Hank's voice just now when he'd mentioned his dad. A loss that monumental had undoubtedly changed his young life and would stay with him for the remainder of his days. Her heart went out to him.

A thick tension crackled in the air as their eyes locked and held. It hummed and pulsed between them like an electrical wire. Suddenly it felt very warm in the squad car. "I should go inside," she said, quickly removing her hand from Hank's and opening the passenger-side door. The crisp air washed over her, and she began to breathe deeply through her nose. The sound of footsteps crunching in the snow alerted Sage to the fact that Hank was following her toward the inn. It made her very happy on Addie's behalf. Girls always needed their daddies!

The smell of baked apples and cinnamon greeted them as soon as Sage pushed open the front door. Following the delicious scent led her right to the kitchen where Trudy was standing with Addie on her hip as she swayed to music blaring from the radio.

Addie's squeals of delight upon spotting Hank were heartwarming. Her little face was lit up like Christmas morning. For the first time Sage noticed dimples on either side of her mouth and two bottom teeth poking through her gums. She was simply precious and Sage thought she might melt right there on the spot.

Trudy held her granddaughter out so Hank could scoop her up into his arms. After pressing a kiss to her cheek, he raised her in the air and playfully jiggled her, causing Addie to let out a series of giggles. The baby reached out a chubby little hand, and Sage wasn't certain who was happier—Hank or Addie. Sage quietly stepped away from the doorway, giving Hank, Addie and Trudy their privacy.

Sage made her way upstairs to her room and firmly closed the door behind her.

After walking over to the closet, she pulled out her largest piece of luggage. She had already taken out most of the contents and placed them in the dresser drawers. After unzipping the suitcase, she dug around in the side compartment and pulled out the item she was looking for. She pressed the blanket to her nostrils, inhaling the familiar scent. Sage had known from the moment Beulah mentioned the owl-themed baby blanket back at the teahouse that she was indeed the missing Lily North.

She no longer had to wonder. The proof was right here in her hands, and it highlighted the fact that her life would never be the same again.

Hank drove back to the sheriff's office after spending some quality time with his daughter. Thankfully his mother managed to distract Addie with a toy lamb when he'd said his goodbyes. It was such a relief to know she wasn't going to fall apart at the seams over his comings and goings. It gave him a boost of confidence. Maybe he really did have a good grasp on this fatherhood role after all!

He felt as if there was a little pep in his step as he walked into the building. Spending precious moments with his daughter left him feeling as if all was right in his world. His entire life was wrapped up in his green-eyed, sandy-haired baby girl. Sometimes it scared him to realize how deeply he loved Addie. If she ever faced any hardships, Hank knew he would do anything to make things better for her. And she better not even think about dating until she was at least thirty years old.

His mind drifted toward Sage. Her encouragement back at the inn meant the world to him. None of his close friends had children, and raising a baby as a single father was brand-new territory for him. Although Sage was still an enigma to him, she seemed to be softening up a little bit. He wished he didn't still have this niggling suspicion regarding her. Had she truly come all the way to Alaska for a getaway?

The door of his office burst open. Connor stormed in, his expression fierce as he said in a raised voice, "You've got to talk some sense into my parents!"

"Whoa. Hold on there!" Hank said, holding up his hands. "What do you have against knocking?"

"I'm sorry, man. Dorinda wasn't at her desk, so I just came through."

Dorinda Clark was Hank's secretary. She was a

stickler for announcing any and all visitors to the sheriff's office. If Connor had dared to rush past her desk in order to get to Hank, she would have put him in his place. Thankfully for Connor, Dorinda had gone home early due to a doctor's appointment.

Connor paced back and forth, full of unbridled energy. With an athletic build, a dark head of hair and classic features, he cut an impressive figure. Along with himself and Gabriel, Connor was considered one of the most eligible bachelors in Owl Creek. In a town with roughly six hundred residents, Hank didn't consider it much of an achievement. He'd known most of the single women in town since childhood. Not a single one truly interested him. If he did somehow venture back into the dating pool in the future, he wanted to feel something special. Sparks. If he met a woman who gave him goose bumps he'd pursue her in a heartbeat.

"There's nothing to be sorry for," Hank responded. "I'd just like to remind you that I actually conduct business in this office from time to time."

His comment caused the sides of Connor's mouth to twitch. They both knew if the walls could talk there would be quite a few stories to be told. Hank's office had become an unofficial gathering place at moments of crisis. Between Gabriel's fiancée having ditched him a few days before the wedding, Hank having found out his ex-girlfriend had given birth to their daughter in secret and Connor's distress regarding the unsolved kidnapping of his sister, there had been loads of drama.

Hank placed his hands behind his head and laid his feet up on his desk. He might as well get comfortable since he had the feeling Connor was about to unload on him. And he didn't mind one bit. It was the least he could do for his lifelong buddy. How many times had he vented to both Connor and Gabriel about Theresa's deception? More times than he cared to remember. He felt thankful that his life had calmed down and he was happily raising his baby girl. God was good!

"Point taken," Connor answered. "I'm just feeling a bit riled up and frustrated. My parents are being manipulated by this anonymous letter writer. It's giving them hope that Lily is alive."

"It's okay to hope," Hank said calmly.

"No, it's not," Connor said in a sharp tone. "After all this time, it's almost cruel to dangle a carrot in front of their eyes."

"I know you want to protect them, but there are some things you can't shield them from."

His friend's expression hardened. "If there's someone out there who's messing with my family, they need to be dealt with before things spiral any further out of control."

"I know it's always been your goal to see that justice is served in this case."

Connor nodded. "I want the perpetrators to be caught and prosecuted. Seeking justice doesn't necessarily mean Lily will come back to us," he said. "You have to admit it's a long shot to imagine it will all work out in the end."

Hank shrugged. "Stranger things have happened. I'm sure you've heard those stories on the news about grown adults who are reunited with their birth parents. And even though it's not likely, I get the impression that your folks need to do something proactively to make them feel as if they haven't given up on Lily."

"None of us have ever given up on her," Connor said, his voice thick with emotion. "Not a day goes by when we don't think about her and what might have been if someone hadn't taken her from us."

"I know, Connor. And I understand it's your nature to be guarded, but don't forget about the information in the letter regarding the baby blanket. That's been a well-kept secret since Lily was taken. The fact that it was in the letter might be the incontrovertible proof your family has been seeking."

Connor ran a hand over his face. He looked a bit beaten down. "You're right. I suppose I need to keep an open mind about it, but I can't shake off this bad feeling that my parents are headed for a world of heartache."

Hank prayed his pal was mistaken. Willa and Nate North had endured every parent's worst nightmare, yet they'd still managed to raise two amazing sons and live a faith-filled existence. After all this time they deserved closure.

"I should probably tell you about what happened earlier with Beulah." Hank made a face. "She was sitting with Sage when I walked into Tea Time. We started talking about the twenty-fifth anniversary of the kidnapping and she told Sage about the baby blanket. I think she was feeling sentimental and it slipped out."

Connor let out a groan. "Granny is way too trusting. She has no idea what someone could do with that type of information. Even after all that's happened to our family, she still believes people are good at heart."

"Come on, Connor. I know you believe that too.

There's no need to worry about Sage. She's not going to say anything to the press or to anyone else for that matter."

The other man rolled his eyes. "How can you be sure of that?"

"I just am. She has kind eyes." Hank wanted to pull back the words right after they flew out of his mouth. Yikes. What was wrong with him?

Connor let out a snort of laughter. Hank realized he'd stepped right into that one. He didn't know why he was jumping to Sage's defense since he still had a few questions about her sudden appearance in town. Perhaps she really was a journalist writing a piece about the Lily North case. Or maybe he was just being paranoid.

"You like her," his friend said with a knowing look. "It's written all over your face."

"I barely know the woman," Hank protested. He felt his cheeks getting red. Connor could always see straight through him.

"Kind of reminds me of third grade when you had a major crush on Clara Tomkins. Even though you wouldn't admit it, Gabe and I saw right through your denials."

Connor knew him like the back of his hand. The good, the bad and the ugly. Hank could deny it all he wanted, but there was something about Sage that tugged at the tender place inside him he'd been safeguarding. He just needed to stuff those feelings down until she returned to her life in Florida.

Connor sat down in the chair across from Hank. "But you'd like to get to know her better. Am I right?"

Hank let out a sigh. "These days I only have room in my heart for one little lady. And her name is Addie Crawford. What's the point in pursuing something when I know it wouldn't go anywhere?" He swung his legs off the desk, sat up straight in his chair and met Connor's gaze head-on. "If you want the plain, unvarnished truth, I think romance is in my rearview mirror. Does it make me happy to say that? No, of course not. But I'm a realist. Been there, done that. I've got the scars to prove it."

Connor let out a low whistle. "You sound even more jaded than I am. Theresa really did a number on you."

"Call it what you like, but I don't have any interest in getting burned again. I'd much rather focus my energies on making sure my daughter is happy and healthy than dodge minefields in relationships." He shuddered. "I've traveled down that road before."

"It has to get lonely though. God didn't intend for any of us to walk through this life alone."

Hank knew there was truth in his best friend's statement, but he also felt strongly about his own position. A long time ago he'd believed in happily-ever-after and a love that would endure all the bad things life threw in one's direction. Having his heart shattered had changed all of that. Being played for a fool had hurt his pride. And for the life of him he couldn't imagine a woman coming into his life who would inspire him to take the plunge again.

## Chapter Six

Sage woke up the next morning to a beautiful Alaskan day. Sunshine streamed through her bedroom window, serving as a reminder that she needed to get up and face the day. She hadn't traveled all this way to spend her time sleeping!

Sage had no idea what she would discover in Owl Creek today, but the very idea of uncovering new facts about her birth family intrigued her. Meeting her grandmother yesterday had been emotionally satisfying even though it had ended abruptly. She really liked Beulah North. If things were different, Sage could well imagine herself sharing many teatimes in the future with the grand dame of Owl Creek. But Beulah had no idea who she really was, and in all likelihood, never would.

A quick look outside revealed a recent snowfall. Everything was covered in a layer of white. It was simply beautiful with the sun glinting against it, creating the appearance of shimmering diamonds. Although Sage wasn't too certain about driving in the fluffy white stuff, she knew it was important to make her own way around Owl Creek without relying on Trudy for transportation. The Owl Creek library was on her to-do list. Surely they would have local records on microfiche regarding the kidnapping. Although she'd read a bit of material from the items found in her mother's belongings and on the internet, Sage wanted to get the Owl Creek perspective. She had goose bumps just thinking about how deeply the kidnapping had affected this small town.

After she had dressed and made herself presentable, she headed downstairs. As she descended the steps, a savory aroma hovered in the air.

"Good morning, Trudy," Sage said as she walked into the light and airy kitchen. Trudy was living proof that this part of the house was the heart of the home. It radiated warmth and goodness.

"Hey there, Sage," Trudy said, turning around and greeting her with a welcoming smile. "I sure hope you're hungry. I've made a bunch of blueberry pancakes, rosemary home fries, reindeer sausage and some scrambled eggs. I used Yukon Gold potatoes which you must try while you're here."

Sage rubbed her stomach. "You're spoiling me, Trudy. I always skip breakfast in the morning, but your meals are too scrumptious to resist. This will tide me over till this evening."

The innkeeper beamed. "I set a place at the dining room table for you, but you're free to eat right here in the kitchen if you like."

"Thanks. I'll sit right here if it's all right. I like the company." Trudy nodded, and Sage settled into a chair.

A gurgling noise caused Sage to turn her head to the side where Addie was standing up in a playpen. She was holding on to the side and smiling at Sage. On impulse, she stood and walked over toward her. She bent over and peered down into Addie's irresistible face. Although she really wanted to scoop her up into her arms, Sage resisted the impulse. She had no illusions about the rigors of raising a baby, but Addie seemed like a sweetheart.

She reached down and swept her palm across the little girl's cheek. Once again, Addie had Sage thinking of things she imagined were years and years in her future. Diapers and Binkies and baby strollers. The smell of baby powder lingered in the air, serving as a reminder of why she'd traveled all this way in the first place. Although Addie was a bit older than she herself had been at the time of the kidnapping, looking into her eyes reminded Sage of all the North family had lost. She imagined they'd loved her as much as Hank adored Addie. Babies were precious gifts.

Although she would never ask Trudy for the details, Sage was incredibly curious about why Hank hadn't known Addie existed until she was three months old. It was none of her business, but she had the feeling there was an interesting story behind it. She couldn't quite put her finger on it, but there was something about Hank Crawford that didn't quite compute.

She sensed a sadness behind the jovial smiles, as if he was masking a world of pain. Had Addie's mother broken Hank's heart?

"Come and get it while it's hot from the griddle,"

Trudy called out, dragging Sage out of her thoughts about Hank.

With a regretful sigh, Sage turned away from the baby and made her way back to the table. Right after she sat back down, Trudy placed a plate overflowing with food in front of her.

"Is this all for me?" Sage asked, chuckling. There was no way in the world she could pack all of this food in, but she sure intended to try.

Trudy patted Sage on the shoulder. "Don't take this the wrong way, but I think you need some TLC. You're an incredible young woman and I can tell you have a lot of heart, but I sense you're going through something difficult."

Sage tried to swallow her food, but raw emotion clogged her throat. She reached for her glass of orange juice and took a sip. Trudy was showing her motherly love and it caused a groundswell of grief to rise up inside her. Despite what her mother had done, Sage loved her. She missed having a mother. And she was still trying to wrap her head around the loss and her stunning deathbed confession.

Trudy held up her hands. "I'm not prying. That's not my way. I just want to let you know you're in a safe place to heal from whatever you're going through. And you can stay here for as long as you like. I welcome the company."

Sage felt such gratitude for being seen by Trudy. Even though her goal had been to keep a low profile while she was in town, it felt comforting to have the other woman acknowledge her pain. She felt so raw and ragged on the inside. It was such a heavy load to bear.

"I lost my mother recently," Sage blurted out. "I'm trying to work through my grief. Some days I feel all right and then other times I feel as if the bottom is falling out of my world."

Not to mention she was having an identity crisis of sorts. All of her life she'd been Sage Duncan and now she had to deal with the reality of being a completely different person.

"Oh, darling, I'm so sorry for your loss," Trudy said, her voice full of sorrow. "No wonder you needed a break from your life back home." All of a sudden, Addie let out a plaintive wail from her playpen. Trudy walked over and picked up Addie, who clutched at her grandmother's shirt as if she was a human life preserver.

Trudy turned back to face Sage. "But I know from my own personal experience that what you're feeling is perfectly normal. It's an up-and-down struggle. It gets better over time, but it never completely leaves you. It's an ache in your soul unlike any other."

"I keep wishing she'd had more time with us. There are so many things I'd like to ask her," Sage confessed. "And now I'll never get those answers."

"That's really difficult, Sage. But I think we all live with unresolved issues. Both of my husbands died unexpectedly, so I've always felt there were so many things left unsaid. I've always tried to focus on the love we shared and not the regrets."

Sage wasn't sure why, but she felt better just for having talked about her mother's death with Trudy. It was so hard to bottle it all up inside and pretend as if everything was right in her world. She was dealing with so many tangled emotions. Trudy was a great listener and she radiated sincerity.

"Thanks for listening. And for understanding.".

"Whoops. I almost forgot. This was placed under the door early this morning. It's for you." Trudy placed an envelope next to her plate. "Maybe you have an admirer." She playfully winked at Sage, who shook her head and chuckled.

Sage picked up the envelope and eagerly opened it. She pulled out a piece of stationery the color of a robin's egg. "It's from Beulah!" she told Trudy, excitement rising up inside her as she read the bold script aloud. "'Please join me at the North Star Chocolate Factory tomorrow for a tour and tasting. Your friend, Beulah North.'" She picked up a sausage and bit into it as she continued to gaze at the letter.

Trudy let out a whistle. "You sure made an impression on Beulah. Don't get me wrong. She's a great lady, but it typically takes some time for her to warm up. Sounds like you made a fantastic impression on her."

"We spent some time together at the teahouse yesterday. She knew my tour of the chocolate factory was interfered with by the press conference and the ensuing mayhem. This invitation is really sweet of her."

"It is, especially since she's going through a tough time." Trudy waved at her plate. "Go ahead and eat up, young lady. Your food is getting cold."

Sage dug into her food with a vengeance. She wasn't sure if it was the Alaskan air, but her appetite had picked up tremendously ever since she'd arrived. Everything tasted wonderful. Once she finished her food, she stood up and walked over to the sink and quickly washed her plate and utensils. Although Trudy always insisted on Sage leaving the dishes for her to clean, she actually enjoyed helping out with chores. It made her feel as if she wasn't simply a paying guest at the inn.

"Trudy, do you think you'll be driving into town today? If so, could I hitch a ride?" she asked. She was still eager to go to the town library and search through the microfilm even though she hated to ask Trudy for another favor.

"Of course you can. I'm taking Addie in for her checkup, so you're welcome to come along and I can drop you off wherever you like."

"That would be perfect," Sage said gratefully. Trudy was such a generous, warmhearted woman, and with each passing day, she was beginning to feel more and more like a close friend. Yet at the same time, Sage felt incredibly guilty about harboring this huge secret.

*You don't have a choice*, she reminded herself. Everything would blow up in her face if she told anyone here in Owl Creek the truth. She'd overheard Connor saying he wanted justice and her father would be the scapegoat. She couldn't allow that to happen. Not in a million years.

On the ride into town, Trudy drove down back roads after meeting up with detour signs on the regular route. It allowed Sage to gain a whole new perspective on the picturesque hamlet. They drove past a bright red-and-yellow little free library overflowing with books. The sight of it made her smile. Suddenly, a large home surrounded by spruce trees came into view. She let out a gasp at the magnificent home. It was a large two-storied log cabin house accented by beautiful stone-work and large modern windows.

"Beautiful, isn't it?" Trudy asked, turning her head toward the grand home.

"It's breathtaking! It looks like it should be on the cover of a magazine."

"That's the Norths' home. Beulah's husband, Jennings, had it built for her after they were married. Their son Nate was raised in that house, and after he married Willa they moved in and raised a family there." Trudy let out a shudder. "That's where little Lily was taken from. Right there on the second floor. The room on the corner."

Sage's palms began to moisten. Her heart was doing somersaults in her chest. It was strange to be so close to the scene of a crime that had drastically altered the course of her life. The rustic home looked so lovely. It was hard to imagine a family had suffered so much tragedy within those walls.

"This town of ours has never really moved past it," Trudy whispered. "I fear we never will."

Her voice sounded so disheartened, as if all hope was lost in ever locating Lily North.

"What if Lily is found?" Sage asked. For some reason she needed to put it out there just to gauge Trudy's reaction.

The other woman kept her eyes on the road and heaved a tremendous sigh. "Oh, Sage, that's what we've all been praying for all these years. But it seems almost impossible to imagine a happy ending after all this time."

"'Now faith is the substance of things hoped for, the

evidence of things not seen.'" Sage recited the verse from Hebrews without even thinking about it. It was one of her father's favorite verses and he'd recited it to her on countless occasions over the years. She couldn't help but think Trudy needed to hear it. Hope was such a precious commodity.

Trudy looked over at Sage and smiled. "Thank you for reminding me that God is always at the wheel. I believe He can make everything right."

Sage bit her lip. Maybe she should've just kept quiet. Was it cruel to give Trudy hope when she knew she would soon be going back home and that the mystery of Lily North's whereabouts might never be known to them? Had it been selfish to come to Owl Creek simply to give herself answers about her birth family? Although the idea of coming clean to her birth family seemed like the right thing to do, the fallout for her father could be catastrophic.

All of a sudden Sage felt as if she couldn't breathe. Everything seemed as if it was crashing down around her. Guilt was eating away at her, bit by bit. What was she doing in this remote Alaskan town? She'd come to Owl Creek seeking answers, but the more she uncovered about the kidnapping the worse she felt about withholding the truth. Could she really go back to Coral Gables and put this all behind her?

The next few minutes passed by with only the sound of Addie babbling in the backseat.

Sage appreciated the lack of conversation since her mind continued to whirl with unresolved questions.

"Can you let me out here?" Sage asked as they came upon the town square. The library was a quick walk from their current location and she felt as if she might scream if she didn't get some fresh air. It felt as if the walls were closing in on her.

"Sure thing." Trudy pulled over toward the curb and placed the car in Park. "Give me a ring later and I'll pick you up."

"You're the best!" Sage said before waving goodbye. She wondered how magnanimous Hank's mom would feel toward her if she discovered the truth regarding her origins. She felt a lurch in her heart just thinking about it. When she'd come up with the plan to visit Owl Creek she hadn't considered meeting people like Trudy who already felt like a treasured friend.

"Focus on the reason you came all this way. You still need answers," she reminded herself as a sudden feeling of resolve gripped her. She began to walk briskly toward the library, feeling a sudden sense of urgency to get as much information as possible while she was in town. Sage didn't want to have any dangling questions or regrets once she returned home. Being here in Owl Creek was a once-in-a-lifetime opportunity.

The town library was a nice-sized, redbrick structure. Sculptures surrounded the exterior. When Sage walked in she noticed beautiful paintings hanging on the walls. They showcased slices of life from Alaska—landscapes, wildlife and landmarks. She felt a serene vibe all around her.

As soon as she approached the circulation desk, a woman with honey-blond hair and gray eyes greeted her. "Hey there. I'm Zoey Thomas, head librarian. How can I help you?"

"Hi, Zoey. I'm Sage Duncan. I'm looking for your microfilm room."

The woman's eyes widened. "You must be Trudy's latest guest at the inn. In a town this size, I knew it was only a matter of time before we crossed paths."

It was really true about small-town gossip. Everyone knew everything that was going on and the very moment a new person arrived. It felt a little bit odd knowing the townsfolk had been talking about her.

"I'm enjoying getting familiarized with Owl Creek. And staying at Trudy's has been a real blessing. She's been incredibly generous."

Zoey nodded her head in an approving manner. "There are lots of good folks in this town. I'm impressed to see you here at the library, Sage. Most tourists never make it inside these walls."

"I'm a schoolteacher, so I figured I would do a little research on the town so I can present it to my class when I go back home." Once again, Sage was only telling part of the story because she knew it would set off alarm bells if she told Zoey she was interested in articles on the Lily North kidnapping.

The librarian came from around the desk and beckoned Sage to follow her. "I'll show you to the microfilm room. It's a quiet day around here so you'll have it all to yourself."

She led her down the hall toward a corridor of rooms, stopping at the second one on the right-hand side. Zoey gave Sage a brief overview of how the system worked before excusing herself.

"If you don't need anything else, I'm going to scoot back to my desk." She shot Sage a wide smile. "Just give me a holler if you have any questions."

"I will," she said with a nod, eager to dig into her research.

Because she knew the date of the kidnapping, Sage was able to hone in on specific dates for her media search. As soon as she entered all the necessary data, results began to immediately show up. None of this information had popped up on her internet search back home. These were local headlines from town newspapers—the *Owl Creek Gazette*, the *Anchorage Press* and the *Alaskan Times*.

"Tragedy unfolds in Owl Creek. Missing baby snatched from nursery. FBI investigates baby's disappearance. Local man named as suspect."

Along with shocking headlines, there were countless pictures accompanying the articles.

One in particular caused Sage to let out a gasp. The black-and-white photo of Nate and Willa North was heartbreaking. Nate had his arm around a sobbing Willa. Even though he was clearly trying to comfort her, they both looked completely shattered. In other photos they appeared shell-shocked, as if they hadn't eaten or slept in days. Another photo caused a groundswell of emotion to rise up in her. It was a photo of a five-year-old Connor holding baby Lily in his arms and smiling at the camera. Sage found herself fighting back tears. What would her life have been like if she hadn't been taken away from Owl Creek? Would she and Connor have been best friends growing up? Sadly, she would never know.

She scrolled by an article detailing the efforts of local law enforcement who were committed to solving the kidnapping. A picture of Sheriff Tug Crawford—

who was the spitting image of Hank—jumped out at her. Sage took out her cell phone and began snapping pictures. Later on when she was in her room back at the inn she could study the pictures further at her leisure. There were so many headlines and images on the screen it felt a bit like information overload. The kidnapping had been splashed all over the newspapers.

After two hours of searching through the files, Sage decided she'd culled as much information as she could from the archives. The newspaper articles revealed the many layers of the tragedy—the pain and angst and turmoil that had reverberated throughout Owl Creek. It hadn't been only the Norths who had been affected. The entire town had been caught up in the tumultuous events. She cringed reading the article about a newcomer to town, Jack Miller, who'd had the finger of suspicion pointed at him before being completely exonerated.

Miller? Was it possible he'd been Piper's father and Trudy's husband? If so, Sage felt truly heartbroken that so many people had been hurt.

She had to be honest with herself. She'd really been looking for something in the files to tie her mother to Owl Creek and the kidnapping. It had been a long shot, but she'd hoped to see her in some of the archived photos so she would know for sure. It still seemed so strange to her to imagine her mother in Owl Creek. For what reason would her mother have trekked to Alaska in the first place?

On her way out of the library, Sage made a point to say goodbye to Zoey, who was just as pleasant as she'd been earlier. She recommended some shops in town for

Sage to visit—a boutique, a pottery shop and a small bookstore. Sage decided to stop by all three stores in the pursuit of a keepsake for her father. He'd called her every day since she'd arrived in Alaska and been very supportive about her mission here in town even though it could cost him big-time if he was ever implicated in the kidnapping. She hit pay dirt when she found a beautiful knitted Irish sweater for him. She'd also purchased a pair of Lovely Boots for herself.

Even though she wasn't terribly hungry, Sage walked over to the diner after shopping.

She really liked Piper and she didn't get many opportunities to see her at the inn due to her work schedule. Maybe she would sit down for a nice cup of cocoa and some French fries.

Once she walked through the doors of the diner, she made a beeline toward Piper, who was manning the counter and conversing with a customer. She had her head thrown back in laughter, her curls whirling around her shoulders. Hank's sister truly was a beautiful woman who radiated from within.

"Sage! It's great to see you here!" Piper exclaimed, her voice sounding animated.

Sage held up her bags. "I've been doing some shopping and getting acquainted with Owl Creek. I know you're busy, but I wanted to pop in and say hello."

"I'm so glad you did." Piper wrinkled her nose. "I love the place, but it's running me ragged. I'm putting in so many hours and not exactly bringing home the bacon if you know what I mean. I'm hoping things will turn around soon."

"Just stick with it. This is a great business, Piper.

The food is fantastic and the vibe is relaxed and comforting. If your mother wasn't such a great cook, I'd eat all my meals here."

"Thanks for the words of encouragement. I've been trying to get Mom to come and work with me, but she loves running the inn. My dad was the original owner here. I've been running the place ever since he passed away. I left everything pretty much the same except for a few little things here and there." A poignant expression was etched on Piper's face. It didn't take a genius to figure out she was thinking about the loss of her father.

Sage reached out and squeezed her hand. "I imagine he'd be mighty proud of you for carrying on his legacy."

"I sure hope so," the other woman said wistfully.

Sage looked behind Piper at the framed photos on the wall. "I love all the photos."

Piper grinned. "My dad put those up. He thought it lent a heartwarming vibe to hang these photos depicting slices of life from right here in town. He took all of them himself."

Sage squinted at one of the black-and-white pictures behind the counter. The photo showed a large group of people standing in front of a church. They were all wearing identical shirts with a colorful logo etched on the front. Suddenly a familiar face leaped out at her. Although she looked incredibly different, Sage knew instinctively it was her mother in the photo. She couldn't have been more than twenty-five or so. Her dark hair was cut in a short bob and she was grinning happily for the photo. She suspected Jane might have been one of the group leaders. Goose bumps popped up on Sage's arms.

Although she had begun to believe she was Lily North, seeing her mother's face staring back at her from a framed photo served as a shock to the system. This was proof positive that her mother had been in Owl Creek at the time of her kidnapping. All this time she had been holding out hope that this had all been one of her mother's delusions. A fantasy of sorts. It hadn't felt entirely real, but with the revelation about the owl-themed baby blanket and this photo of her mother, she had to accept the truth. She *was* Lily North. Her mother had come to Owl Creek as part of a youth group and had stolen her from her birth parents, Willa and Nate North.

How in the world was she supposed to process this information? And why had the smiling young lady in the photo resorted to stealing another woman's child? Clearly, she had never known Jane Duncan at all.

A feeling of dizziness gripped her. Her head was spinning like a wheel. She felt her knees giving out on her. Just as she sensed herself falling, strong arms enveloped her. Sage held on for dear life so she didn't wind up on the diner's parquet floor. When she looked up at her rescuer, she found herself gazing into Hank's concerned blue eyes.

# Chapter Seven

Hank held Sage tightly against his chest with his arms encircling her. The moment he'd seen her body swaying, his protective instincts had kicked into high gear. Thankfully, he'd been heading over to the counter to say hello to her and Piper, which put him within striking distance to catch her fall.

"Are you all right?" he asked, his heart thundering in his chest. Although Sage looked as pretty as ever, her color was a bit off and she seemed to be breathing heavily.

"I'm fine if you don't count my embarrassment. I don't know what happened. All of a sudden I felt so light-headed." She moved away from Hank so that he was no longer holding her. He felt strangely bereft. He watched as she sat down on one of the stools at the counter.

"Here's some ice water," Piper said, holding out a glass for her. "You might be dehydrated."

Sage reached for it with a trembling hand. Hank intervened, reaching for the glass and raising it toward her lips. She was shaking so badly he wasn't sure the glass wouldn't slip from her hand. She took a few sips, then pushed it away. "Thanks. I'm good."

"Did you eat today?" he asked with a frown.

"Yes," Sage said with a firm nod of her head. "Trudy made me a world-class breakfast. I'm fairly certain my stomach is still full."

Hank chuckled. "Why doesn't that surprise me? Cooking is her superpower."

Sage giggled. "I can well imagine it is. I can still taste those blueberry pancakes melting in my mouth."

They both laughed for a moment and Hank felt reassured by Sage's light mood. She no longer looked unwell. He knew his mother would have heard about the dizzy spell by dinnertime and he'd be peppered with a million questions. Even the slightest tidbit of news traveled fast in Owl Creek.

"Hank, why don't you take Sage over to that booth table by the jukebox? It's a lot more comfortable than these stools," Piper suggested. "I'll send someone over to take your order."

Sage sputtered. "It's okay, Hank. You don't have to babysit me. I'm fine."

He lowered his head and said in a conspiratorial manner, "Little sisters can be pretty fierce. When Piper tells me what to do, I tend to listen."

The smile Sage sent in his direction threatened his equilibrium. He couldn't remember the last time a woman had made him feel so completely off-kilter.

Once they settled into the booth, Hank didn't waste any time following up on his questions regarding her episode.

"So, do you often get dizzy like that?" Although he didn't want to pry, Hank wondered if she was suffering from a medical condition. Perhaps that's what she had been hiding. He still couldn't rid himself of the notion of there being more to Sage Duncan than met the eye.

Sage shook her head. "Never. Perhaps it's the change in climate. Or dehydration like Piper suggested." She shrugged. "I feel a lot better now."

"Hey! Sorry I'm late." Hank looked over to see Gabriel standing at their booth. He'd totally forgotten about his lunch plans with his best friend. The incident with Sage had thrown him a bit off course.

"Hi there," Sage murmured in a friendly voice.

"Hello. I'm Gabriel Lawson. You must be Sage," Gabe said, sticking out his hand to shake Sage's.

"Yes. Sage Duncan. Nice to meet you, Gabriel."

"I hope I'm not interrupting anything." Gabriel jerked his thumb in Hank's direction. "I was supposed to be meeting this guy for lunch, but it seems he's forgotten all about me." Gabe smirked at him.

"I didn't forget," Hank said, feeling annoyed at Gabriel for absolutely no reason he could fathom.

"Please sit down. If anything, I'm the one who's barging in here." Sage scooted over to make room for Gabriel. Hank felt a strange sensation as he watched his buddy sit down next to her. It was the oddest thing— he loved Gabe like a brother, but it felt as if he was horning in on his time with Sage. It left him feeling befuddled. Sage was a sweet and beautiful woman, but he didn't have a claim on her. So why did he feel so out of sorts?

"I hope you're enjoying your time in Owl Creek,"

Gabriel said. How had Hank forgotten how charming his friend could be around females? Throughout their lives everyone had loved Gabe for his winning personality. Connor had been known for his classic good looks while Hank himself had been viewed as the proverbial boy next door.

"Owl Creek is a great town," Sage responded, a slight smile hovering at the corner of her lips. "Frankly, I hadn't expected all of this commotion. The brochures I read said it was a quiet Alaskan town."

Gabriel groaned. "Tell me about it. This morning when I went into Java to get a coffee, a journalist was waiting by the door with a microphone and a camera crew barraging me with questions about the Norths' reward. I'm getting really good at saying *no comment*."

"Has there been any progress?" Sage asked. "Were they able to track down who wrote the letter?"

"Not unless you consider hundreds of calls from charlatans as progress. There were no fingerprints on the letter and it was postmarked from New York City, so it's a dead end," Hank answered. "Offering monetary inducements doesn't usually bring out the best in people." The information about the letter had already been released to the media, so he knew he wasn't revealing any tightly kept secrets.

"I'm sure Willa and Nate did what they thought best," Gabriel countered. "It's easy for all of us to judge, but they're in a tough spot."

"I wasn't judging," Hank snapped. "I was making an observation based on my professional experiences."

A sudden tension bristled between them. Sage nervously twiddled her fingers and looked down at the menu. Hank and Gabriel locked eyes across the table. The vibe between them was off. Just then, their waiter, Dexter, showed up at the table and the focus shifted toward placing their orders. Light conversation ensued until their orders came. Gabe regaled them with tales of his bush pilot adventures while Sage talked about her second grade students. Hank added a few anecdotes about being sheriff in a small town.

"I hate to eat and run, but I have to meet Trudy down the street. She's giving me a ride back to the inn. I'm going to go take care of my tab at the counter."

Gabriel stood up from the table so she could exit. "It was really nice to meet you, Sage," he told her. "Enjoy the rest of your day."

"Thanks, Gabriel," Sage said. "It was a pleasure to meet you, as well." She turned toward Hank. "Thanks for the rescue earlier. I really appreciate it."

"It was nothing. Bye, Sage," he replied with a nod, his eyes trailing after her as she walked away.

Once Sage left, Gabriel didn't hesitate to put him on the spot.

Gabriel frowned at him. "What's going on with you?"

Hank took a long sip of his coffee. "I don't know what you're talking about," he said, placing the mug down on the table.

"Are you kidding me? You were glaring at me from the moment I sat down. You should have just told me to leave if you wanted to make it a lunch date with Sage."

"I'm not dating Sage," Hank said through clenched teeth. "Matter of fact, much like yourself, I'm not going out with anyone. Nor do I intend to."

"Hank, you won't always feel this way," Gabriel said

in a gentler tone. "As you well know, my own heart has been kicked around, but I haven't given up on finding someone to walk through life with. When the timing is right it'll fall into place."

He let out a snort. "You're beginning to sound like a greeting card."

Gabriel rolled his eyes. "Why am I wasting my breath? Between your moods and Connor's, I don't know if I'm coming or going. Must be something in the water," he grumbled, taking a long swig from his own coffee cup. "I should just stay up in my plane and avoid human contact."

"Did something else happen with Connor?"

Gabriel's tense expression spoke volumes. "He's really upset about the press conference. For quite some time now he's been intent on finding the person who took his sister, but now all he wants is to put it in the past." He made a face. "He plans to ask his parents to rescind the reward offer and to stop looking for Lily."

On her way out of the diner Sage had been within earshot of Hank and Gabriel's conversation. Gabriel's voice had been animated when he'd told Hank about Connor's wish for his parents to stop their search for her. At first she couldn't believe her ears. How could her brother want to give up on being reunited with her? How could he ask Nate and Willa to make that earth-shattering decision?

Her emotional reaction to the news left her feeling stunned. She made her way outside, shivering as the cold blast of arctic air hit her squarely in the face. Hot tears stung her eyes and for a moment it had felt as if she couldn't breathe. She never would have believed it would hurt so much or that she would feel so betrayed. In her heart she'd wanted reassurance and the knowledge that her birth family was doing fine all these years later. But knowing they might soon give up on her caused an ache in her soul.

It was such a strange reaction since this entire time it had been her wish to remain anonymous so she could protect her father. There was no getting around the fact that being here in Owl Creek was a game changer. On paper the North family had been a remote entity, tied to her by DNA but not necessarily anything else. But researching the tragedy and seeing their desperation up close and personal changed everything. It didn't feel so black-and-white anymore; there were so many shades of gray in this situation.

Sage knew there were no easy answers. Should she approach Willa and Nate and beg them for mercy? What would happen if she pulled Connor aside and told him the truth about why she'd come to town? Maybe Beulah would help her sort it all out. And maybe she was living in a dream world. These people had suffered pain and loss for over two decades and had finally reached a breaking point. It was naive to believe everything could be fixed simply by confessing her true identity.

As she waited for Trudy in front of the post office, Sage prayed for this feeling of hurt to subside. She didn't want raw emotions to sway her off course.

*Dear Lord, please help me with all of these feelings threatening to consume me. I'm trying to hold it together, but it's becoming more and more difficult.*

*Please soothe my soul so I can continue to figure things out and make sense out of what happened all those years ago.*

At the end of a long day, Hank found himself once again seated at his mother's dinner table. Lately he found himself eating at Trudy's inn more than usual. Although he tried to tell himself it had nothing to do with Sage, he knew better.

"Thanks for dinner, Mama. Let me help you clear the table." Hank stood up and began to gather the dishes.

Ed Walters, a visiting journalist who hailed from Los Angeles, smiled at Trudy and said, "Thank you, Trudy. Your home cooking reminds me of my own mama's meals, may she rest in peace."

"Hey, Sage. Would you mind holding Addie while I help in the kitchen?" Hank asked. "She'll probably fall asleep once she settles into the crook of your arm. I can tell by her drooping eyelids she's tuckered out."

Sage looked hesitant. "I don't know, Hank. What if she fusses? I'm not that experienced with babies. I'm not sure I'd know what to do if she wails."

"You'll be fine, Sage. Addie likes you," Trudy said with an encouraging nod.

Sage gingerly lifted Addie from Hank's arms and began to rock her back and forth. He almost laughed out loud at the terrified expression on Sage's face. For a schoolteacher, she seemed a bit intimidated at the prospect of holding Addie as she settled into sleepy time.

He followed behind Trudy as she headed toward the kitchen. They stood side by side at the kitchen sink and set about the business of washing and drying the dishes. It brought to mind memories of growing up in this household and performing this chore almost every night of the week. When Piper had gotten old enough, she too had joined in.

"I'm so glad you were at the diner when Sage had her dizzy spell. Piper said you really saved the day. My son the hero," Trudy said, nudging Hank in the side.

He shook his head. Leave it to his mother to label him as heroic. She had a tendency to make him better than he was. "Hardly. All I did was give her a shoulder to lean on."

"Handsome and humble. That's my boy!" Trudy crowed. "Thanks for helping me clean up. I know it's almost Addie's bedtime."

"It's the least I can do since you watched Addie again for me and took her to her doctor's appointment."

"I'm her grandma, Hank. It's in the job description," she said in a teasing manner. "Not to mention being one of the joys of my life."

Hank leaned over and placed a kiss on her cheek. "We're blessed to have you, Mama. I appreciate you and Piper more than you'll ever know. I just wish she didn't have to work so hard at the diner. I barely get to see her anymore."

Trudy wiped her hands on a dishrag and let out a little sigh. "You know she's determined to carry on Jack's legacy. That diner was his pride and joy, along with the two of you kids. I wish that I could help her out more over there."

Silence descended over them for a few moments. Losing his stepfather, Jack, had been a huge blow to their family, and none of them had recovered from it, least of all Piper. She hid her pain under a thick facade, but if you looked long enough you could see the telltale cracks. For Hank it had served as another tremendous blow to lose a father figure so unexpectedly.

"By the way, Sage has been asking me about car rentals, but in a town this small it's a real head-scratcher. With all the journalists in Owl Creek they've scooped them all up. I suppose I sound ungrateful since they're paying customers, but all the media attention has me on edge."

"Let me see what I can do. I might know someone who can help her out," Hank offered.

"Oh, that would be wonderful. She's a real delight. Beulah invited her for a tour of the chocolate factory tomorrow. I just can't tell you how sweet and helpful she's been. It's so nice having someone like Sage staying here." She glanced over at him and raised an eyebrow.

Hank frowned at Trudy. "Mom, stop giving me the side-eye. You're doing it again."

"Doing what?" she asked, her voice full of innocence.

"Playing matchmaker. Fess up. You're trying to set me up with Sage."

"I'm not doing any such thing." She winked at him. "Now if the two of you struck up a close friendship, I wouldn't object."

Hank couldn't help but chuckle. Some things never changed. His mother considered herself to be a matchmaker, although she'd never successfully set up a single couple. "There's something about her that seems a bit off to me."

"Off? In what way?"

He shrugged, then struggled to put his feelings into words. "I don't know, Mama. I think it's a bit peculiar she landed in Owl Creek. It's not exactly a hot spot for tourists this time of year. I don't really buy her story. She seems a bit jittery at times."

Trudy made a tutting sound. "Hank Crawford. I'm mighty proud you took up after your daddy and became town sheriff, but you are one of the most suspicious people I've ever known. You need to give it a rest. Not everyone has a malicious agenda."

He looked at his mother and wiggled his eyebrows. "And you trust everyone on face value. In my humble opinion she seems a bit secretive. Maybe she's a journalist writing a story about the twenty-fifth anniversary of the kidnapping and she's trying to dig up some dirt."

"Your theory makes no sense. Why would she hide her profession? There's no crime in being a journalist," she snapped. "Didn't your friend Boone Prescott marry a writer?"

"Yes, he did. And she went to his town under false pretenses," Hank said in a raised voice. Grace Prescott was a lovely woman, but she hadn't been transparent at all until her deception had backfired. "Maybe I should run a background check on Sage."

Trudy swatted her hand in his direction. "Hush before Sage hears you. You'll do no such thing, Hank!" She shook her head at him, disapproval radiating off her in waves. "It's not my place to tell you this, but Sage's mother passed away a few months ago. She's grieving the loss, and from what I gather, a bit overwhelmed with life at the moment. She came to Owl

Creek to disappear for a while and to reflect." She scowled at Hank. "Cut her some slack."

All of a sudden, Hank felt like a colossal jerk. More than most people, he understood how grief could pull you under. Although he'd only been six years old when his father died, the loss had plunged him into a deep sadness. Losing his stepfather, Jack, in an accident four years ago had been another huge kick in the gut. Jack had been a wonderful father, husband and stepfather, and had treated Hank as his very own.

He had been reeling in the aftermath of Jack's death and coming apart at the seams. That period had lasted until he'd discovered he was a little girl's father. At that point Hank had made a decision to embrace fatherhood and walk a righteous path. He'd accepted God into his life. All for the love of his little girl who deserved an honorable, responsible father.

"I didn't know that she'd lost her mother," he said in a small voice. He felt horrible about being so suspicious of Sage when she was in the throes of grief.

"I for one know what she's going through. I was widowed at twenty-seven, then widowed again at forty-eight." His mother's eyes misted over. "Both times it brought me to my knees."

Hank's heart plummeted at the sight of his mother in tears. "You've been through the wringer, Mama. You've had more than your fair share of pain and loss."

She let out a brittle-sounding laugh. "But guess what? I still believe in love. I still think it's possible for me to find another person to walk through this life with by my side. Some might say I'm crazy, but I call it belief."

Hank leaned over and placed a kiss on his mother's cheek. "I'm sorry. I didn't mean to dredge up all of these painful memories."

"There's no need to apologize, Hank. Loss is part of living and loving. And if I had to do it all over again, I'd still love your dad and Jack with every fiber of my being even though losing them gutted me. I've been twice blessed, and I wish you believed in love the way I do. It's a gift from God. Believing in something you can't touch or see, but you know is real all the same is a beautiful thing indeed."

She wiped tears away from her face with the back of her hand. "What Theresa did to you was terrible, but you can't continue to hide your heart away because you fear it might get broken again. That's not living your life to the fullest."

"I'm not hiding it away. Between my work and raising Addie, I don't really have a lot of free time to put my feet in the dating pool."

"Whatever you say, Hank!" Trudy let out a snort and shook her head. "Why don't you go relieve Sage? I'm sure Addie is sound asleep or ready to go down for the night."

Hank hesitated. He hated to see his mother upset and he felt guilty because it was all his fault. He opened his mouth to apologize again, but Trudy shooed him out of the kitchen. He sensed she wanted to be alone with her memories.

When Hank headed back into the living room he stopped abruptly in the doorway and soaked in the sight of Sage sitting on the couch cradling a sleeping Addie in her arms. She was lightly running her hand down his daughter's cheek in the slightest of caresses. Addie's innocent face was turned upward toward Sage.

So much for not being good with babies, Hank thought wryly. She looked like a natural.

Seeing the two of them snuggled up together caused a feeling of longing to rise up inside him. Because of his past with Theresa, he had never really dared to dream of having it all—more children, a mother for Addie and a wife to have and to hold. It had been almost instinctual to stuff down those longings to prevent himself from getting hurt again.

But, Hank realized, it was almost impossible to change who he was as a person even if he worked overtime to pretend as if those things didn't matter. Ever since he'd been a little kid, he had wanted a family of his own. And, if he was being honest with himself, he still did. Lovely, sweet Sage was bringing all those emotions to the surface. Suddenly he was thinking about what it might be like to be with someone like her, to allow himself to care about a woman the way he'd once cared for Theresa. Those dreams had been cut short by her betrayal.

Hank shook off the tender feelings. He didn't know Sage Duncan, just like he hadn't ever truly known Theresa. She had given birth to his child in secret and made a colossal fool of him. If she hadn't tragically died in an accident, he may never have been informed about Addie. That knowledge still stung like crazy.

Sage lifted her head so they made eye contact. A tender smile was etched on her face. He knew it had everything to do with his spectacular baby girl.

He moved toward her, trying his best not to make a sound as he approached. If he could put Addie in her car seat without waking her up, she would stay asleep for the rest of the night.

"She really is the sweetest baby I've ever seen," Sage whispered, her gaze veering back toward Addie.

"I like to think she takes after me," he said in a teasing voice.

"I think she's really fortunate to have you, Hank," Sage murmured. "Your devotion to her is crystal clear."

"We're blessed to have one another," Hank said, warmed by Sage's words. God had been good to him by bringing Addie into his life. It had changed his world for the better in so many ways. Hank regretted being intimate with Theresa outside the confines of marriage, but he could never feel bad about the little charmer who was the most important thing in his world.

He reached out and gently took Addie from Sage's arms. A little sigh escaped Sage's lips as he made the transfer. Being so close to her was a dangerous thing, as he'd discovered earlier at the diner. She smelled of vanilla and a flowery scent he couldn't quite place. The more time he spent in her presence, the more appealing she seemed. As it was, he found himself thinking about her at random moments during the day. He surprised himself by wondering what her favorite flowers were and whether she liked anchovies on her pizza.

He focused on placing Addie in her car seat as a diversion from staring at Sage. For a moment he simply gazed at his baby girl, safely nestled in her carrier. Before he knew it, Sage was at his side, reaching down and placing Addie's blanket over her, along with her stuffed giraffe.

"There's a fierce wind out there," she said, wrapping her arms around her middle and shivering. "We wouldn't want her to catch a chill."

"No, we wouldn't," Hank said, feeling a sudden urge to stay a bit longer. "Well, good night then."

"I'll get the door for you," Sage offered, walking ahead of him toward the front entrance.

As Hank walked out into the cold Alaskan night, he resisted the urge to turn around and take one last look at Sage. He imagined she looked lovely illuminated by the soft glow of the front porch lantern. So many thoughts were rumbling around in his head as he drove the short distance home. All of his professional instincts were warning him that something was off with Sage, yet his heart was pulling him in her direction. Despite his firm resolve to have nothing to do with the beautiful schoolteacher, Hank was having a difficult time ignoring the deep-seated yearning he felt every time she was in his orbit.

# Chapter Eight

Sage woke up the following morning filled with excitement and a bit of trepidation about her tour of the chocolate factory. Last night before she went to bed she'd looked at Beulah's invitation and smiled at the sweet tone of the older woman's words. It meant a lot to be embraced by the North family's matriarch. Spending time with her grandmother was the biggest inducement to attend the tour, although chocolate was a runner-up. This would be a wonderful opportunity for her to check out the North family business and to get better acquainted with Beulah.

She practically wolfed down her breakfast as Trudy looked on with a bemused expression on her face. After eating, Sage headed back upstairs to look in the full-length mirror. She wanted to look her best upon meeting up with Beulah. She imagined there wouldn't be many opportunities for her to spend time with her, so she wanted to make the most of it. A moment like this would be cherished for a lifetime when she went back home.

"Sage! Your ride is here," Trudy called out from downstairs.

Sage grabbed her purse and headed down. "My ride?" she asked in a surprised voice. "I thought you were my ride."

Trudy was grinning from ear to ear. "Hank is outside waiting for you. He found a vehicle for you to use while you're in town."

She felt her jaw drop. "Are you serious? That's great news, Trudy! It's awfully kind of him."

Trudy nodded her head. "If you haven't noticed, Hank is a gem." Sage carefully avoided Trudy's gaze. She had the feeling Hank's mother was on a fishing expedition. Although the sheriff was a perfect example of an Alaskan hunk, Sage wasn't going down any romantic roads while she was in Owl Creek. She didn't want to give Trudy the slightest bit of encouragement. On the other hand, she didn't want to be rude.

"I'm mighty grateful," she murmured, wanting to acknowledge Hank's kindness for finding her a vehicle. Trudy rewarded her with a huge grin.

Sage put her parka on and shoved her feet into a new pair of Lovely Boots she'd purchased yesterday in town. As Trudy had promised, they made her feet feel as if she was walking on a cloud. "Bye, Trudy. I'll catch you later!" Sage rushed outside into the frigid winter morning. Hank was standing beside a red truck parked in front of the house. Astro was sitting in the back of the truck as if he was looking forward to getting a ride. Sage quickly swallowed up the distance between her and Hank.

"Trudy told me you found a vehicle for me to use. Is

this it?" she asked, jerking her chin in the direction of the truck. She was smiling so hard it made her cheeks hurt. She couldn't think of the last time anyone had done something this sweet for her.

"It's all yours for the duration of your stay here in town. It's seen a few miles over the years, but it'll get you where you need to go. All you have to worry about is putting gas in it when it runs low. I filled the tank up for you so you won't need to refuel for a while."

"Let me know how much I owe the owner."

Hank waved a hand in the air. "Don't worry about it. He owed me a favor. It's yours to borrow for as long as you like, no strings attached."

"Oh, Hank, it's all so wonderful." A feeling of immense gratitude washed over her. Sage threw her arms around Hank, enveloping him in a tight bear hug. He smelled like pine needles and apples—a warm, pleasant scent. Although she knew her enthusiasm might seem over-the-top, she couldn't rein herself in. Everyone here in Owl Creek had been so kind to her ever since she arrived. She hadn't expected this treatment at all by the townsfolk. Hank was a busy man—a single father and a town sheriff—who didn't have to go out of his way to help her.

When she pulled away from him she couldn't help but notice he seemed a bit flustered.

It was kind of nice seeing another side of the always-in-control sheriff.

"Thanks so much for making this happen," she gushed. "Trudy has been wonderful, giving me rides, but I like being independent. I hate feeling like a burden. She already has a lot on her plate."

"That's understandable, although I know Mama doesn't think of it that way. She loves spending time with you. I think it's safe to say you're her favorite guest of all time."

Sage let Hank's words settle over her like a cozy blanket. It was such a heartwarming feeling to be embraced so enthusiastically by Trudy. It was making her feel as if she really did belong in Owl Creek. Because in truth, she wasn't really an outsider. This quaint town was where she'd been born, where her family had planned to raise her before the bottom had fallen out of their world. This Alaskan town was beginning to feel important to her in so many different ways.

"That means a lot to me," she acknowledged, biting her lip to keep herself from tearing up. These days it felt as if she was on an emotional roller coaster. Ever since the death of her mother, Sage felt like all the nerve endings in her body were exposed.

"My truck is parked back on Main Street, so why don't you get behind the wheel and drive us into town," Hank suggested. "We should get going. I wouldn't want you to be late for your tour with Beulah. Just take it nice and easy since you're not used to snow-packed roads."

Sage nodded and seated herself behind the wheel while Hank motioned for Astro to jump down from the back of the truck. She felt a bit nervous about driving in such wintry conditions, but having Hank by her side in the passenger seat gave her a boost of confidence. It seemed as if nothing bad could happen on his watch. He radiated an air of calm authority, alerting her to upcoming curves in the road or slick patches to watch out for. It felt nice driving a truck since it was bigger and sturdier than her small coupe back home.

"Should I drop you off at the sheriff's office?" Sage asked as they came upon Main Street.

"No. It's not necessary. I can walk over. Take the left on Forrest and then the factory will be straight ahead on your left," Hank instructed. Sage followed his directions, and within a few minutes, the factory rose up to greet them. It was a large brick structure that didn't quite fit in with the small-town vibe. Although she'd gotten a look at it the other day, her nerves had been all over the place and she hadn't really taken in any of the details.

Sage parked in the designated lot and turned toward Hank.

"That wasn't so bad," she said, letting out a sigh of relief. "Other than a few slippery spots it was pretty straightforward."

"I'm impressed," he murmured, nodding approvingly. "Don't forget it gets dark early, so you might want to head back to the inn while there's still daylight."

"Good point." The last thing she needed was to get lost on a dark and remote Alaskan road with caribou and black bears running around. Being in Owl Creek was an adventure, but she wasn't looking for that type of excitement. "Thanks again for setting me up with the truck so I can explore on my own without bothering Trudy."

"You're quite welcome. To be honest, you've given me an excuse to go inside," he said, his expression sheepish. He reached into the backseat and held up a loaf of home-baked bread inside a cellophane bag with a bright red bow on it. "I have a peace offering for Beulah. Pumpkin is her favorite."

"You bake?" Sage asked, delighted at the notion of the handsome sheriff making baked goods in his kitchen. She wasn't used to meeting many men who were accomplished bakers. Hank Crawford really was a Renaissance man.

He appeared to be pleased with himself. "I sure do. Trudy wasn't sending out a son into the world who didn't know how to fend for himself." He let out a little groan. "She said it was her duty to my future wife."

Sage tried to stifle her giggle, but she couldn't stop the sounds of mirth coming from her mouth. The more she tried to rein it in, the louder she laughed. Hank joined in on the laughter and the truck was filled with sounds of merriment.

"We'll be having our annual Owl Creek cook-off competition soon. You won't want to miss it. I think I'll give Mama and Piper a run for their money and make my famous corn bread."

"I'd like a front-row seat for that competition," Sage told him as images of Piper, Hank and Trudy vying for the trophy danced in her head. She found herself looking forward to it.

"Ready to go in? It's about that time," Hank said, tapping his watch.

Sage rubbed her hands together. She felt like a little kid. "Yes. I'm so excited. I feel like Charlie going to Willy Wonka's chocolate factory."

"Just don't go falling into any chocolate rivers,"

Hank quipped, the corners of his mouth twitching with amusement.

"I could think of worse things," Sage said, enjoying the playful banter. What was the harm in it? She knew there was no hope of anything further happening between them. Getting involved with the sheriff of Owl Creek would be like putting her hand too close to the fire. The stakes were way too high and she wasn't in a place to explore the chemistry between them. She already felt as if she was teetering on a high wire with no safety net. Adding Hank to the equation would be disastrous.

When they got out of the truck and headed toward the steps leading toward the entrance, Beulah was standing at the door to the chocolate factory waving at them. Hank looked over at Sage and smirked. "If I hadn't seen it with my own eyes I wouldn't believe it. Beulah really has taken you under her wing, hasn't she?"

Just hearing Hank confirm what she'd been thinking caused a sliver of worry to pass through her. Was she being foolish to get so close to Beulah? Was it fair to come to the chocolate factory under false pretenses?

The joyful expression on Beulah's face caused Sage to stuff down her worries. After everything she'd been through, Beulah deserved as many happy moments as possible. If Sage could provide a little bit of joy to her long-lost grandmother, she wouldn't hesitate to do so.

Beulah quickly ushered them inside from the cold. Once they were in the building, Beulah turned toward Hank with a raised brow. "What brings you here, Hank?"

He leaned down and pressed a kiss on Beulah's cheek. Sage detected a smile quirking at the corners of her lips.

"I missed you, Beulah. And I come bearing a gift." Hank held out the pumpkin bread.

Beulah frowned. "Are you trying to bribe me, Sheriff Crawford?"

"Not at all," Hank said. "Just trying to win a little favor with you."

"You know pumpkin bread is my weakness," Beulah said, leaning in and giving Hank a peck on the cheek. "Even the best of friends have spats. My faith reminds me to forgive rather than to hold on to things."

Hank placed a hand over his heart. "Then my work here is done!" he proclaimed. "You two ladies enjoy yourselves. I need to head to the sheriff's office." With a wave of his hand, Hank disappeared out the door. Sage felt her gaze trailing after him.

After he'd walked out of the building, Beulah looked at her and said, "A girl could do a lot worse than Hank Crawford."

"I imagine so," she responded, feeling a bit wistful about Beulah's comment. Hank was the type of man who inspired devotion. She knew it was only a matter of time before he fell for a local woman and settled down. That's how things worked, especially in small towns like Owl Creek. Hank wasn't the type of man who should walk through life without a loving partner by his side. She tamped down the discomfort she felt knowing it wouldn't be her. The two of them might have a connection, but there was no way in the world Sage could afford to explore it.

Beulah rubbed her hands together. "Let's get started on the tour. There's a lot to see at the North Star Chocolate Factory, if I do say so myself." Sage chuckled as the older woman ushered her down a long corridor and immediately began telling her about the history of the company.

Two hours later and Sage's head was spinning with all the information she'd discovered about running a chocolate business. She'd had no idea how many steps were involved from turning a cocoa bean into a piece of chocolate. Beulah had shown her all areas of the factory, including the production line, the wrapping and packaging room, as well as the area where the cocoa beans were sorted, winnowed and roasted. There were so many things to see—the storage tanks, large pieces of machinery, the huge mound of cocoa beans. And of course, the finished product, the chocolate itself! Loads and loads of delectable confections.

Along the way there were lots of stares and smiles from the workers. Most were probably wondering who she was and why she rated a private tour with Beulah North. It didn't bother her at all. Strangely, she felt right at home in the chocolate factory.

"Why don't we go to my office?" Beulah suggested. "I have a few treats for you in there to take with you."

"That's so thoughtful of you," Sage gushed. Beulah treated her as if she was a very important person. It made her feel all warm and fuzzy inside, as if she truly mattered.

"It's my pleasure. I recall you saying milk chocolate was your favorite, although there's quite an assortment."

"I'll never say no to chocolate," Sage said, linking

arms with Beulah. Once they entered her private office, Sage almost stopped dead in her tracks at the sight of her birth mother standing near Beulah's large mahogany desk. Willa's face was in profile as she riffled through some papers, and for the first time Sage observed a slight resemblance between herself and Willa. There was something about her jawline and the slope of her nose. It was an eerie feeling to be standing so close to the person who had brought her into this world. And even more surreal that Willa had no idea Sage was her daughter.

"Willa! I didn't know you were here today!" Beulah exclaimed.

Willa looked up from her paperwork and grinned at her mother-in-law. "Yes. Nate and I had a meeting with some distributors who flew in from Anchorage," she explained. "I was hoping to catch you so I could go over this paperwork with you. We can do it another time, since I see you have a visitor."

Willa North was a beautiful woman with luminous skin and wide blue eyes. She radiated a sweet vibe. Although at first glance she appeared to be frail due to her petite body type, Sage knew her biological mother had to be a strong woman to have endured such trauma and heartache. Being in such close proximity to Willa made her pulse skitter. It was disorienting to come to terms with the fact that this was the woman who'd given birth to her and nurtured her for the first few months of her life.

"I'd like to introduce you to my friend Sage Duncan. She hails from Florida and she's visiting Owl Creek for a few weeks. I invited her here today so I could give her the grand tour." Beulah winked at Willa. "She's a big chocoholic."

"That's just what we like to hear around here." Willa smiled at Sage, dazzling her in the process. She felt a little bit like a deer caught in the headlights. Her legs were shaking so badly she wasn't sure how she was still standing. She walked over and stuck out her hand. "Sage. What a lovely name. Welcome to our chocolate factory. Any friend of Beulah's is a friend of mine."

Sage shook hands with Willa. The moment their skin touched a strange sensation flowed through her. Perhaps she was being fanciful, but she truly felt a special connection between them. She wondered if Willa felt it too?

"Take a seat, Sage," Beulah said, waving her toward a love seat. "We can sit for a while and have some hot chocolate, which is a specialty of our company. Come join us, Willa." Beulah picked up the phone on her desk and put in the request for the hot cocoa to be delivered to her office.

"I'd love to," Willa replied, following behind them and sitting down next to Sage. Suddenly Sage felt a bit self-conscious. She really wanted Willa to like her. All of a sudden she felt like the shy ten-year-old she'd once been, nervous about being popular with her peers. This moment felt so important, as if she'd been waiting her whole life for it, without even knowing it.

While Beulah was ordering refreshments, Sage sat side by side with Willa, who showed her all the different types of confections Beulah had placed in a large basket for her.

"A lot of people don't care for chocolate-covered

cherries, but they're my favorite, bar none. I could eat a whole box myself," Willa said with a giggle.

"They're one of mine too," Sage admitted, laughing at the thought of Willa devouring a whole box of the confections.

By the time the hot cocoa and cookies came, Sage felt like they were fast friends. Willa seemed fascinated by the idea of living in the Sunshine State and the differences between the Alaskan and Floridian climates. Sage was able to ask Willa about the various owls the town was known for. She told Sage about an upcoming town event called the owl walk where all the residents ventured into the woods to get a glimpse of all the town's owl species in their natural habitat.

"I look forward to it most of all because my father-in-law, Jennings, always makes an appearance," Willa explained. "We call him our resident ornithologist since he knows everything about dozens of bird species, owls in particular."

There was something comforting about being in Willa's presence. She'd had a similar experience on her first meeting with Beulah at the teahouse. Never in a million years had Sage imagined she'd be sitting here with her mother and grandmother chatting and enjoying hot chocolate.

All she'd truly hoped for in coming to Owl Creek was to get a few answers to some burning questions about her identity. Although she'd resisted the truth ever since her mother confessed about the kidnapping, a part of Sage had instinctively known it was all true. She hadn't really needed the baby blanket to prove it. There had always been a little part of her that hadn't felt as if she fit in as a member of the Duncan family. Although she'd always loved her parents, Sage had always felt as if a piece of her hadn't belonged. Although she'd attributed it to being adopted, she now knew it had been far more complicated.

In the deepest regions of her heart, Sage wanted to know that the members of her birth family were happy and that they'd thrived despite the tragic events of twenty-five years ago. By finding this information out, she could finally move on with her life and put her mother's shocking confession in the past. However, all of a sudden the decision to leave Owl Creek without revealing herself as Lily North didn't seem so simple. Now that she was up close and personal with her family members it seemed like an impossible dilemma. Who knew what the future might hold with her Alaskan family? The possibilities were endless.

Just then Nate North strode into the room, bringing with him a vibrant energy. "There you are, my love. I've been looking all over for you." He strode over to his wife and pressed a tender kiss to her lips. Sage couldn't look away from the sight of them.

Beulah sent Sage a knowing look. "These two lovebirds have been together since their freshman year in college. Nate, this is Sage Duncan. Sage, this is my son, Nate."

Nate frowned. "Hello, Sage. Have we met before? Your face looks familiar to me."

Her heart skipped a beat. Was it at all possible Nate was responding to her on an instinctual level? Her stomach was twisted up in knots. "I—I was at the factory the other day when you had your press conference, but I left due to the crowd. Maybe that's why I look familiar?"

Nate still looked puzzled. "Sure. Maybe that's it," he said, sounding unconvinced.

Without warning, Sage felt her good mood plummet. Things were getting way too intense. Nate and Willa were the epitome of Alaskan sweethearts. She couldn't seem to drag her gaze away from them as they held hands and looked lovingly into each other's eyes.

Their child had been ripped away from them and yet they still adored each other. They'd suffered one of the most devastating traumas a couple could withstand and somehow they had emerged on the other side, still in love. Still committed to one another. It left her awestruck. And it spoke to her about the enduring nature of true love.

All of a sudden it all came crashing down around her. She was standing in a room with three people who were related to her by blood, yet they didn't realize it. It felt so wonderful yet incredibly wrong at the same time. She was so terribly conflicted. What would God think about her actions?

A passage from John 3:18 came to mind. She'd been reading the Bible ever since she was a child and this particular verse had been used by her father to teach her right from wrong. At the moment it resonated with her.

*My little children, let us not love in word, neither in tongue; but in deed and in truth.*

Truth? It had always been so important to her, yet she'd been dodging it like a minefield ever since her arrival in Owl Creek. And now she had to sit in her own reality. Didn't her birth parents deserve to know what she'd discovered? Was it fair to make them suffer for a lifetime?

When it was time to leave, Sage reached out to Beulah and Willa with tight hugs. She held on to Willa for an extended period of time, realizing she might never get this opportunity again to embrace her mother. She smelled of roses and chocolate and pure goodness. Sage felt at home in her arms, and when Nate took Sage's hand and pressed a kiss to her knuckles in an old-fashioned gesture, the emotions bubbling beneath the surface could no longer be contained. She blinked away tears, knowing she could never explain them in a million years. It was a lonely feeling being the only one in the room who fully understood the significance of this moment.

Beulah walked Sage to the entrance and gave her one last hug. "Thanks for coming out and spending time with me today. It meant a lot." Sage nodded and squeezed Beulah's hand. She didn't trust herself to utter a single word of goodbye. It was only a matter of time before she broke down completely.

When Sage turned around to take one last look at the chocolate factory, Beulah was still standing there waving in her direction. She raised a hand in farewell, then turned back around and made her way over to the truck with tears streaming down her face. Thankfully she was facing away from Beulah. After getting in the vehicle she sat for a few minutes as the engine warmed up. She'd made a big mistake in seeking out her birth family. Nothing felt cut-and-dried anymore.

The thought of leaving Owl Creek and never seeing them again tore her up inside.

Willa, Nate, Beulah, Trudy, Piper and Hank were living, breathing people who had burrowed their way into her heart. And now that they were there, she had no idea how she was going to erase them from her mind when she returned home.

## Chapter Nine

It was shaping up to be a beautiful night for the owl walk in Chinook Woods. The heavily forested area had been a fixture for Hank ever since childhood. It had been a place of exploration and discovery for him. He'd always been fascinated by the wildlife in the woodlands—foxes, deer and on occasion, caribou. The owls had always been the most interesting to Hank, however. They were mysterious creatures who could see in the dark of night, at which time they were most active. It was fitting that the town had created a winter event highlighting the natural beauty of the magnificent birds.

It seemed to Hank as if the whole town had turned out for the event. He had made it a point to keep away from the inn for the last few days. Instead of staying over for dinner, he'd cooked at home for himself and Addie or met up with Gabriel and Connor at Piper's diner. He'd figured out that the best way to keep Sage at arm's length was to limit the time he spent in her presence. Seeing her all the time was only serving to imprint her on his mind. Yet, despite his best intentions and the deliberate actions he'd taken to avoid her, thoughts of Sage still lingered. He couldn't get her out of his mind for the life of him.

When his gaze scanned the crowd, he instantly spotted Sage. She was chatting with Zoey Thomas. With her cream-colored hat and gray scarf, Sage looked warm and stylish. He looked down at her feet. She was wearing a sturdy pair of Lovely Boots. It made him smile that she'd heeded his mother's suggestion. She really was getting the lay of the land.

Sage had driven herself, Piper and Trudy over to the woods this evening. Piper had told him Sage wanted to be able to navigate at night if she needed to, so this served as a test run. She'd surprised him by displaying such pluck and grit. Driving in Alaska wasn't for the faint of heart. As a Florida girl Sage clearly didn't have much experience driving on snow-slickened roads, but she was careful and confident.

It was nice to see her making friends here in town, even though she wasn't going to be a permanent fixture in Owl Creek. The idea of not seeing her sweet face for much longer caused a pang in the region of his heart. He was being ridiculous, he told himself. He'd only known her for a few weeks and as it was, didn't fully trust her. Maybe she was in a bad marriage and running away from an abusive situation. The very idea of it caused all of his protective instincts to go on high alert.

Maybe he was completely wrong about Sage. Perhaps he was making her pay the price for Theresa's lies and deceptions. Mama had told him he was allowing the past to color his future. But what was he supposed to do with all of his festering doubts? He hadn't told a soul that he'd had a few niggling suspicions about Theresa back in the day, but his feelings for her hadn't allowed him to listen to his gut instincts.

And he'd paid a hefty price for his lack of awareness.

"She's some kind of wonderful, isn't she?" Piper asked, sidling up to him.

"Who?" Hank asked, feigning ignorance.

"The lady you've been trying not to stare at ever since she arrived," she said, chuckling.

Hank reached out and tweaked her nose. He'd been doing it to his little sister since they were kids even though he knew it bugged her.

"Ouch!" she cried out, swatting his hand away. "Stop trying to divert my attention away from the fact that you're gawking at Sage."

"Sage is a nice woman."

"Nice, huh?" Piper let out an indelicate snort. "Is that your way of saying you're interested in her?"

"You're getting way ahead of yourself, sis. She's only here for a few weeks and I'm not looking for anything romantic. I've got my—" he began.

"Yeah yeah yeah. You've got your hands full with Addie. You're beginning to sound like a broken record." Piper rolled her eyes. "Go on and talk to her," she said, nudging Hank in the side. "You know that you want to."

Hank scowled at his sister. "If you don't stop being so pushy you might end up in a snowbank."

Piper let out an outraged squeal. "Those are fighting words, Sheriff!"

She picked up a handful of snow and began making a perfectly rounded snowball.

"You wouldn't dare!" Hank said in his most forbidding voice. "It will not end well for you if you go down that path. That's a solemn promise."

Before Piper could respond, Hank felt a hard object smack against his chest. When he looked up, Sage was standing a few feet away from him, with a grin stretching from ear to ear on her face.

Hank sputtered. "Oh, I get it! Girls against boys, huh?" he asked, advancing toward Sage with a throaty laugh.

"I've got your back, Sage," Piper cried out as she raced toward Hank and began pummeling him with snowballs. He held up his hands in surrender. "Let's call a truce."

Sage placed her hands on her hips. "What do you say, Piper? Can we cut him a break?" she asked.

His sister put a finger on her chin. "Hmm. Perhaps we can strike a deal with him. If he promises to go get us some hot cocoa, we'll grant him a reprieve."

"That sounds very fair to me," Sage responded, giving Piper a thumbs-up sign.

"I promise! I promise! That's an easy compromise," he said, wiping snow off his parka.

Sage walked over and flashed him a playful grin. "No hard feelings, right?"

"Of course not! All things considered, I got off pretty easy. Two hot cocoas coming up," he said, walking over toward the concession stand. All proceeds from tonight's event went toward wildlife conservation efforts in Alaska. It was an endeavor near and dear to his heart.

He loved animals of all kinds. At one point as a kid he'd aspired to be a large-animal veterinarian, although those dreams had taken a backseat to his desire to pursue a career in law enforcement. Nevertheless, he always made it a point to volunteer and contribute to animal-protection efforts. He couldn't imagine Alaska without caribou, moose or threatened species such as polar bears.

Hank found himself whistling a cheerful tune as he stood in line. A festive mood hung in the air and everyone seemed to be in a joyful frame of mind. Including him. He was *truly* happy…and had so much to be thankful for. His daughter was content and healthy. He'd found his groove as a single parent. Piper was living out her dream of running Jack's diner. Trudy was moving past her losses and thriving. And despite his reservations, spending time with Sage made him feel good. Getting pelted with snowballs had never been so fun. He almost felt like a teenager with his first crush, and he wondered if Sage had picked up on it despite his efforts to play it cool.

Once he'd purchased the drinks, Hank headed back to the area where he'd left Sage and Piper. As he got closer he spotted Gabriel standing with them.

"Look who I have here. The prettiest girl in Owl Creek," Gabriel said, holding Addie in his arms with the utmost care. She was reaching up and grabbing his chin, which was a surefire sign she was crazy about him. Her diaper bag was slung over his shoulder. "Trudy asked me to watch her while she helped out with the arts-and-crafts table. Her expertise was needed over there." There was so much going on around them—music, arts, education, food, entertainment. It was a fun-filled Owl Creek evening that made him feel proud of his hometown.

Hank grinned at the sight of Gabriel and Addie. "I can take her if you want to grab some refreshments," he offered.

"Are you kidding me? Uncle Gabe hasn't been able to spend time with Addie in quite some time. It would be my pleasure to watch her while you check out the owls." He smiled at Sage. "Prepare yourself to be blown away. You'll never view owls in quite the same way again."

Hank held out the cups of hot chocolate for Piper and Sage, who quickly took them off his hands.

"I've really been looking forward to it!" Sage exclaimed, her cheeks rosy from the cold.

He had the feeling Gabriel was paving the way for him to be alone with Sage. There was a hint of mischief etched on his face, and he was whispering to Piper. Hank had seen that look dozens of times ever since they were little kids. Gabe had a wide-open heart as big as Kachemak Bay. It touched him to know his friend wanted him to find love even though he was reluctant to pursue it in his own life.

"Why don't you and Sage set out on the trail? I'll wait for Mama," Piper suggested.

Gabriel and Piper exchanged a loaded glance that made Hank even more suspicious. Hmm. Was Piper in on it too? Were these two conspiring to play matchmaker?

"Sure thing. We'll keep an eye out for you," Hank said. "Shall we?" he asked, turning toward Sage, who couldn't contain her excitement. She'd come a long way from the closed-off woman he'd met on the ferry. She was opening up like a chrysalis turning into a butterfly. She'd always struck him as beautiful, but now he was seeing the true essence of Sage Duncan. There was so much more to her than met the eye.

As they walked along the wooded trail illuminated intermittently by path lights, they filled the silence with conversation. It flowed easily between them with no awkward silences or forced chatter. There were plenty of other townsfolk walking in the woods, but it felt as if it was just the two of them. Even if there couldn't be anything romantic between them, they could still be friends, couldn't they? He wasn't certain he could view her solely in that way, but he would try his best.

"Gabriel is so sweet with Addie. He seems to really love kids," Sage remarked. "You're blessed to have a friend like that."

"He's crazy about little ones. He and Addie are two peas in a pod. He's her honorary uncle, as well as Connor. In my opinion, a girl can never have too many protectors. Both would take a bullet for her. I don't say that lightly either."

"I'm surprised he doesn't have a house full of his own kids."

Hank heaved a tremendous sigh. "He intended to, but his fiancée ran out on him a couple days before their wedding."

Sage let out a shocked sound, then raised her mittened hand to cover her mouth. "That's awful, Hank. I can't believe it."

"I shouldn't have mentioned it, but it still sticks in my

craw that a woman could have treated him so poorly. It was three years ago, but it feels like yesterday."

She shivered. "That's not something a person would get over very easily."

"He hasn't. Not even a little bit. Rachel was a hometown girl, born and bred right here in Owl Creek. It surprised everyone." Honestly, Hank wasn't certain Gabriel would ever completely move past Rachel's desertion. He knew all too well about being blindsided. It tended to make a person bitter and unwilling to put themselves out there to get hurt again.

"I guess we all have our scars, don't we?" Sage asked, staring directly at him.

Hank narrowed his gaze as he looked at her. "Mama told you what happened between Addie's mother and I, didn't she?"

Her eyes widened and she shook her head. "Of course not. Trudy would never betray your confidence like that. She's a grizzly-bear mama. I'm pretty sure she thinks you're a superhero."

He chuckled. "That's what mothers are for, I suppose. They're fiercely protective of their cubs." He let out a beleaguered sigh. "The details are widely known here in town so I've got nothing to hide. All the townsfolk were front and center watching it unfold. Addie's mother and I dated for almost four months. Her name was Theresa. She came into Owl Creek like a whirlwind, full of vitality and beauty. Honestly, I'd never met anyone like her in my entire life. I fell completely head over heels in love with her."

"It sounds very romantic," Sage said wistfully.

"Until it wasn't," he answered. "Theresa came to

Owl Creek under false pretenses. She'd cooked up some scheme to extort the North family under the guise of pretending to be Lily North. She was clearly using me to get close to them. I discovered she had a handful of arrests for petty larceny and running scams all over the state. When I confronted her she took off to parts unknown. Then, about a year later, I received a phone call from one of her friends telling me that she'd died in a car accident." He shuddered as cold swept across the back of his neck. "Finding out about Addie blew me away. I had no idea."

Sage couldn't hide her surprise. She sucked in a deep breath and bit her lip. "I can't imagine how devastated you must have been. And hurt."

"As a result, I can't abide lies or liars. What kind of person tries to take advantage of a family like the Norths who've lived out their worst nightmare?"

Sage appeared shaken. Her mouth opened, then closed. Perhaps she thought he was being harsh about Theresa, but considering all the pain she'd caused him, he wasn't about to give her a pass.

Hank had surprised himself by opening up to Sage about his past. Usually, he was more guarded with his private life. However, there was something about being here with her in the woods on the owl walk that made him feel as if he'd known her all his life. She seemed truly interested in his past and the circumstances that led to him raising Addie on his own.

He felt a slight tremor pass through him, remembering all the different emotions he'd gone through. Surprise. Fear. Betrayal. And grief for the woman he'd once loved. At the time he hadn't been sure if he would make it through all the turmoil in one piece. But once again, God had lifted him up and shown him a light at the end of the tunnel—Addie.

*Fear thou not; for I am with thee.* Hank had recited that particular verse dozens of times during his most challenging hours. It served as a reminder he wasn't alone even in the darkest of moments. God always walked beside him.

"I suppose I've never felt worthy of my own love story, so I wasn't surprised when things fell apart with Theresa, but it really stunned me that she didn't think I deserved to know about my daughter."

Sage squinted at him. "Come again? Why on earth wouldn't you be worthy of love?"

He shrugged, feeling a bit on the spot. He'd slipped up by admitting those feelings to Sage. How did he even begin to answer that question? It was an insecurity he'd been struggling with for a long time. Perhaps it went all the way back to when he'd lost his father. He wasn't good in relationships. They always fell apart for some reason or another.

"I don't know exactly. But it's what I felt at the time with Theresa. I think she sensed it too. Exploited it even. She knew I didn't feel as if I deserved the happy ending."

Sage stopped walking and simply stared at him for a few moments. Finally, she spoke.

"I've only known you for a short time, Hank, but I do know you're so very deserving of love. You're wonderful and kind. You're generous to a fault. And I've seen the loving way you treat Addie, Trudy and Piper, not to mention the sweet nature of your relationship with Beulah. If you're not worthy of romantic love, I don't know who is. Any woman would be blessed to win your love and affection."

Hank let out the huge breath he'd been holding. His chest swelled with emotion. No one except Trudy had ever said anything remotely like this to him. And that was a mother's job, to build up her child. "Thank you, Sage. I appreciate the vote of confidence more than you'll ever know." It meant the world to him to hear such praise from Sage's lips. He was blown away by her generosity of spirit.

"I only spoke the truth," she said in a soft voice that tugged at a place deep inside him.

As they locked gazes something fluttered and pulsed in the air around them. The chemistry sparking between them was incredibly powerful. Overwhelmed by what he was feeling, Hank struggled to find a way back to mundane topics.

"So, what do you know about owls?" he asked, shifting the focus away from their unspoken connection.

"Very little, matter of fact," Sage answered. "I know they're nocturnal animals and I watched a documentary once where they were shown as hunters."

"Right on both accounts. They hunt at night and their vision is pretty spectacular, as well as their hearing."

"I imagine that helps them gather food in the darkness," Sage noted. "And predators probably have a hard time seeing them at night."

"Are you sure you haven't studied owls before?" Hank teased, earning himself a giggle from Sage. He loved seeing her lighthearted moments. She was even more beautiful when she showed her joyful side.

"I promise you I haven't," she quipped, making a funny face that did nothing to diminish her beauty.

Hank stopped in his tracks and pointed at a nearby tree. "And right there are the most magnificent owls you'll probably ever see. Snowy owls are known for their coloring and the fact that unlike most owls, they are active during the day. So they are at rest right now and you won't see them flying around or looking for prey."

"Wow! I've never seen one up close. They're stunningly beautiful." Sage's voice was filled with awe.

"They truly are," Hank said, thinking they weren't nearly as stunning as she was. He wasn't at all certain Sage knew her appeal. From where he was standing, she seemed humble and unassuming. She barely wore any makeup and she didn't seem self-absorbed in the slightest. In so many ways she was a breath of fresh air.

For a moment Hank completely forgot everything he knew about snowy-white owls. Sage had the kind of eyes a person could get lost in. She was gazing at the owls with such a look of wonder on her face it made his heart swell. It felt as if he was experiencing it for the first time, even though he'd been around these creatures his whole life. So much for staying in the friend zone with her. He wasn't sure it was possible.

He cleared his throat, willing himself not to think about such things.

"The town's founding families named it Owl Creek once they realized it was inhabited by one of the largest populations of owls in the United States," he explained.

"That's pretty fascinating. What I know about owls

wouldn't fill a postage stamp, but they're beautiful creatures. The sounds they make are really interesting."

"Their hoots can be heard for miles. When I was a kid I used to go out in our backyard to try to track down owls because it sounded like they were right outside the door. Boy was I disappointed when Trudy explained that they could be miles away."

Trudy had been a wonderful mother to him. She'd worked really hard to compensate for the fact that his father wasn't around. In many ways the strength she'd shown as a single mother gave him inspiration on a daily basis with regard to bringing up Addie.

"What type of owl breed is that? I've seen it before." She pointed up at a tree where two gray-and-white owls were sitting on a branch, their onyx-colored eyes blinking fast and furiously.

A tall man with sunken-in cheeks and brilliant blue eyes turned toward them and explained, "Those are barn owls. They're easy to remember because of their heart-shaped faces. Those owls are the most common ones not just here in Owl Creek but around the world."

"Sage, this brilliant man is none other than Jennings North, Beulah's beloved husband and partner in crime. Jennings, this is Sage Duncan. She's visiting Alaska for a few weeks," Hank said, feeling delighted by the sight of Beulah's husband. As of late it was a rare occasion when Jennings ventured out and about. Perhaps he was finally taking steps to move past the tragic events of twenty-five years ago.

Jennings tipped his hat in Sage's direction. "Nice to make your acquaintance, Sage. Are you the young lady that Beulah showed around the factory the other day?"

"Yes, I am," Sage said. "It was incredibly generous of her to invite me. She made me feel right at home."

"She's taken a shine to you. That's for sure. She was as pleased as punch you decided to spend the day with her." There was a slight tremor in his jaw. "It took her mind off a lot of unpleasant things."

Hank thought he saw tears pooling in Sage's deep brown eyes, but upon second glance he thought he might have imagined it. "I'm happy I could do that for her," she murmured.

"Me too," he said. "If you'll excuse me, I'm going to join up with that group of middle schoolers over there. I know they have a hundred or more questions about these owls. It seems they're going to be tested on it at school tomorrow."

As Jennings walked away, Sage's gaze trailed after him. He couldn't be sure, but it seemed as if she'd wanted a little more time in Jennings's company. It endeared her to him since he considered Jennings North one of the most compassionate and wise people he'd ever known. He always included him in his prayers in the hope he might find some measure of peace.

"He seems like a sweetheart, but his eyes are full of shadows," Sage observed.

"Yeah, that about sums it up. He's never moved past Lily's abduction. He hasn't been the same since that terrible night," Hank explained. "I think he deals with a lot of guilt because of the success of the chocolate company. He wonders if it made his family a target."

Sage gazed at him with mournful eyes. "It's hard to deal with such an inexplicable loss. It's bad enough when someone you love passes away, but to have someone taken away from you like that without warning is catastrophic."

Hank seized the moment. It was the perfect time to offer Sage his support and compassion. "I should have said something before tonight, but I wasn't sure how to bring it up. I know why you're here in Owl Creek, Sage."

# Chapter Ten

Suddenly it felt as if all the air had whooshed out of her lungs. Her worst fear had come true.

Hank knew she was Lily North! She broke out in a sweat despite the cold chill in the air. Panic began to rise up inside her. How in the world was she going to justify her actions? There was no way she could make him understand, especially after he'd just told her about Theresa's grand deception. He probably would consider her to be a fraud. The very thought of it made her knees go weak.

*Please, Lord. Help me make it clear to Hank why I'm here in Owl Creek.*

"I—I can explain," she began. "I came here seeking answers."

Hank held up his hand. "You don't owe anyone an explanation." Hank shifted from one foot to the other. "Trudy told me about your mother's passing. I'm so sorry. Losing a parent is incredibly painful. Of course you needed some time to process it. You wanted to get off the grid so you could grieve the loss."

Her heart landed with a thud in her belly. Relief coursed through her. Hank didn't know anything about her link to the Norths. Her guilty conscience had risen to the surface and she'd panicked. She sucked in a fortifying breath. Her secret hadn't been exposed after all.

"Thank you," Sage murmured. "It's hard to believe she's really gone. She'd been sick for a while, but death is so final. There are so many things I wish I could ask her. So many unanswered questions."

"Were the two of you close?" Hank asked.

The question was a loaded one. Sage wasn't sure she could ever aptly describe the relationship between them. On some days it had felt as if her mother was her best friend while at other times they would argue over the slightest thing. She now believed Jane had carried around a lot of guilt with her because of the kidnapping. Her culpability had trickled down and affected their rapport.

"Not particularly," she answered. "We weren't at a good place when she died. To be honest, more times than not we were at odds." She shivered, then wrapped her arms around her middle. "We were very different."

"Any siblings to lean on?"

"No, Hank. I'm an only child, which makes the grieving even more difficult. It's just me, Dad and Aunt Cathy. He was such a devoted husband to my mother. This has really hit him hard."

"I know a little about that. I was only a little kid when my dad passed, but I remember my mother's grief felt like a tidal wave capable of pulling us under. Ultimately, his death ended up bonding us together. It was the two of us against the world until Piper and my stepdad Jack came along."

"You and Trudy have a great relationship. I don't think my Mom and I ever had that type of connection. The truth is, I never really understood her. She was very mercurial—her moods were all over the place. I suspect she had a mental illness, but it wasn't something ever discussed in our household." She sighed. "As a child it frightened me because I never knew what was coming around the bend. But in her own way she loved me fiercely. It was a complex situation, to say the least."

"That must have been really hard for all of you," he murmured softly. "Maybe she was afraid to be completely honest with you out of a fear of rejection. A lot of people hide their struggles due to the stigma."

"I see that now, but it made things difficult between us, particularly when I was a teenager. There were a lot of things left unspoken between us when she passed." She couldn't voice it to Hank, but she desperately wanted to know why her mother had abducted her. How could she have lived out her days knowing she'd committed such a terrible act?

Ever since her mother's death, Sage had been wondering why she hadn't broken down and cried. Perhaps it had been the shock of her mother's deathbed confession. She'd been straddling a line between grief and disbelief, but now, it felt as if all of her nerve endings were on fire. Letting out a strangled sob, Sage covered her face with her hands. At long last, all the emotions she'd been bottling up inside were coming to the surface.

"I'm so sorry, Sage. I didn't mean to make you cry."

She felt Hank's strong arms encircling her. He pulled her toward him and she wept against his chest. The scent of pine filled her nostrils and she inhaled deeply. Hank smelled like the great Alaskan outdoors. His embrace made her feel safe and secure. She wanted to hold on to him and never let go. Perhaps then all of the pain would dissipate.

"It's not your fault. I'm way overdue. I've been holding in a lot of these emotions and trying to shoulder my way through the grief." She wiped away her tears and sniffled. "It just hurts so much knowing we'll never get the opportunity to truly clear the air."

"But you loved each other. That's the important thing." He was patting her back and speaking to her in a comforting tone.

Hank was right. Even though he didn't know about her mother's heinous actions, his words still applied. No matter what her mother had done, she'd loved her. And she always would. Nothing could truly ever change that fact. She might never forgive her for altering the course of her life and stealing her from her rightful family, but she couldn't erase the love she'd always nurtured in her heart for her.

Sage ducked her head down and nodded. "I loved her very much. And I miss her." She breathed in the cold air through her nose, giving herself a little jolt. "Sometimes it shocks me to realize I can't just pick up the phone and call her. It's like there's this hole in my heart where she used to be. And even though things were far from perfect between us, she was still my mother."

"God only gives us one mother," Hank said. His eyes radiated kindness.

Sage felt her lips tremble. His words were incredibly ironic. He had no idea that life had given her two mothers. One had been robbed of the opportunity to raise her while the other one had been a very flawed mother with an explosive secret in her past. She didn't want to be anything like the woman who had raised her, yet here she stood incapable of being open and honest with Hank.

For so long now Sage had been straddling the line between truth and deception.

Looking into Hank's eyes made her feel ashamed of all the secrets she'd been harboring. He was a good and decent man who made his living enforcing the law. From everything he'd told her about his past, there was no doubt in her mind that deceit and dishonesty were off-limits.

What if she opened her mouth and confessed who she really was? Would Hank take her under his protective arm and help her tell the North family about the circumstances leading to her trek to Owl Creek? Would he lend her his unwavering support? Or would he react with disgust and dismay? Perhaps he would think she was a horrible person for not coming clean the moment she'd gotten off the ferry.

*I can't abide lies or liars.* A little while ago he'd made things quite plain with his statement. It gave her chills to recall the intensity in his eyes when he had uttered those words.

In her heart Sage wanted to believe everything would be all right if she spilled the truth. But the situation was so complex. And she had landed smack-dab in the middle of it, steeped in her mother's deception.

Yet again it was abundantly clear that she needed to keep quiet about her ties to the North family and the town itself. She didn't want to run the risk of losing Hank's goodwill. It was probably selfish of her, but she didn't want to ruin the moment by making such an explosive admission. Just for tonight she wanted to push it to the back of her mind and simply enjoy all that Owl Creek and Hank Crawford had to offer.

Hank reached out and swept a few snowflakes off Sage's rosy cheeks. He didn't see how it was possible, but she looked even more radiant than usual. When she'd started to cry, he had pulled her off to a side trail where onlookers wouldn't be able to witness her raw emotion. In a town like Owl Creek gossip spread like lightning and he didn't want Sage to be the topic of flapping gums.

Little beads of moisture dotted her sooty lashes, leftover remnants from her tears.

"Alaska suits you, Sage Duncan." He let out a sigh. "You might just be the prettiest woman Owl Creek has ever seen."

She ducked her head down, the hint of a smile playing around the sides of her mouth.

"That's mighty fine praise, Hank. I'm not sure if I deserve it, especially with a tearstained face."

"I'm simply speaking the truth. Tears can't diminish true beauty."

Sage was beautiful inside and out. Her revelations this evening made him see her with a more generous heart. What he'd viewed previously as her being cagey could have been signs of deep mourning for her mother. He felt ashamed of himself for being so wary of her. His tumultuous history with Theresa had really impacted his ability to trust women. Mama was right. He was walking around with the shadows of the past following him.

*Lord*, he prayed. *Please open up my heart and mind so I can treat people with a wide-open spirit instead of always being guarded. I know it's wrong to judge yet I'm constantly finding fault with Sage. I don't want to be guided by fear and suspicions.*

He had a long way to go before he conquered his issues from the past, but asking the Lord for assistance felt like reaching out for a life preserver. Although he pretended everything was fine with him on a day-to-day basis, he knew he wasn't living his best life. He was jaded due to his prior experiences. The shell he'd built around himself had been born out of heartache, but tonight had shown him that little by little Sage was chipping away at it. She was stirring up feelings he'd stuffed down for a long time.

*You'll never know if you don't try.* It was something his father used to tell him. Whether it was trying out for the Little League baseball team or working to put together a massive Lego set, those words of encouragement had been thrown in his direction.

Tug Crawford had been a bighearted, generous man who had loved freely and without reservation. Hank had always wanted to live up to his dad's larger-than-life image. He had always imagined he could do so through his career in law enforcement. Perhaps another way of doing so would be to put himself out there with Sage despite his reservations.

He wanted to kiss her. Truthfully, he had wanted to kiss her for quite some time now, but his desire to steer clear of complications had veered him off course. His head had ruled his emotions. And why shouldn't he share an embrace with a lovely woman with whom he'd established a special connection? This opportunity might never crop up again. Sage would be leaving town soon and he would be left with a host of regrets if he didn't at least try to act on his instincts.

Hank dipped his head down and pressed his lips against Sage's. Her sweet aroma filled his nostrils— a mixture of a floral scent and the hint of evergreen. Her lips were soft and tasted like the hot cocoa she'd just finished. Once his lips touched hers, he knew there was no going back. He was stepping out on a limb of faith and going for it. She kissed him back with equal intensity, her lips moving tenderly against his own. He felt her clinging to the fabric of his winter coat as if he was literally sweeping her off her feet.

This embrace was the culmination of every moment, every thought he'd ever had about this fascinating woman since he'd first seen her on the ferry. When they pulled apart, Sage's face was still upturned toward his own. When she opened her russet-colored eyes they were shining brightly. If he could, Hank would have stretched this moment out a bit longer. He drew in a ragged breath to steady himself. Kissing Sage had been a dizzying experience, one he'd thoroughly enjoyed.

When they returned to the main path, they walked side by side with their arms touching.

Along the way they were met with a few raised eyebrows and curious glances. Hank smiled to himself at the notion that he and Sage would be on the lips of the townsfolk tomorrow morning. Normally, he would hate being the subject of gossip, but strangely, this didn't bother him at all. Maybe this was progress, he realized.

Perhaps there was hope for him after all.

As the night wound down, Sage settled herself by the roaring fire in order to warm up her chilled bones. The temperature in Owl Creek gave a whole new meaning to the word *frosty*. She'd been all right for most of the evening, but her nose and cheeks now felt frozen. Sitting by herself gave her the opportunity to reflect on her romantic interlude with Hank. The kiss had been enjoyable, even though it hadn't been the smartest move on her part. Hank Crawford represented truth and honor. If he had a single clue as to the secrets she was keeping, he would be full of outrage and condemnation. And she wouldn't blame him. Not one single bit. It made her feel awful just knowing she was keeping things from him, especially after Theresa had put him through the ringer. She let out an anguished sigh. She shouldn't have kissed him! It only served to complicate matters.

Her chest tightened at the thought of Hank's disapproval if he knew her truths. She hadn't planned on caring about him; it had happened when she'd let her guard down. Sharing a kiss with Hank had been emotionally satisfying and romantic, yet it wasn't going to amount to anything other than a moment in the moonlight. There wasn't a future for them. She'd be leaving Owl Creek soon, and she would take this beautiful memory with her, all the while regretting lying to him.

She raised her fingers to her lips, reliving the sweetness of Hank's kiss. If only she could truly explore this incredible connection with Hank without so much hanging over her head. She might regret not being able to do so for the rest of her life. Forgetting Sheriff Hank Crawford would be near impossible. But a life with him was as far out of reach as the constellations in the dark Alaskan sky.

Suddenly, Willa appeared, taking a seat by the fire next to Sage. The presence of her birth mother was comforting. She exuded such an air of grace and tranquility. Sage remembered reading about Willa's and Nate's faith in one of the old newspaper articles. They had talked about how their belief in God had led them through the darkness and allowed them to still believe in the light. It had given her chills when she'd read it.

"Hey there, Willa. I was hoping to see you here tonight," Sage said, excitement roaring through her at being able to spend a little time with her mother.

"Hi, Sage. I hope you're enjoying yourself." She leaned over and gave Sage a hug. "This is one of my favorite town events. There's such a feeling of goodwill in the air. It's palpable."

"I really am having a good time. Your owls are magnificent." Sage studied Willa's face.

Despite her cheerful words, her eyes were blank and lifeless. It was as if Sage was looking at a completely different person than the one she'd spent time with the other day. Something seemed very off.

"I don't mean to pry, but is everything all right? I

know this is a stressful time for you, so it's understandable if you're not feeling your best."

Willa's lips trembled. "Oh, Sage. I'm feeling completely out of sorts. I don't know if I'm coming or going if I'm being honest." She let out a ragged sigh. "My family has made a decision to rescind the reward offer, and it's breaking my heart."

Sage felt a roiling sensation in her stomach. Although she'd known it was a possibility, it felt a bit shocking to hear it from Willa's lips. "The one you and Mr. North offered for information about your daughter's whereabouts?"

"Yes," Willa said, blinking away moisture in her eyes. "Nate and I have had such a single-minded focus on tracking down Lily that we neglected to consider the heavy toll it's taken on Connor and Braden, not to mention Nate's parents.

"Neither of my boys has had an easy time of it," she continued. "I think we need to focus on their wants and needs. My son Braden is always making excuses for not being here in Owl Creek with the family. Connor thinks he's running from something. Growing up in the shadow of Lily's abduction has been difficult to say the least."

Nausea rose up in Sage's throat. She felt sick. Her birth family was suffering due to her.

Although it hurt to know they were giving up on finding her, she understood their need to let go. They had been in limbo for twenty-five years. It was time.

She swallowed past the lump in her throat. "Well, you clearly love your family very much. Protecting the ones we love is so important." It was what she was doing with the man who'd raised her. Come what may she would go on protecting him, even if it meant she might never be known as Lily North.

"It is, isn't it? I'll never stop loving my Lily and praying for her health and happiness, but I've got to let go of this idea she'll come back to us."

Sage locked gazes with Willa. The emotional side of her wanted to cry out and tell her mother the truth. But the rational side of her knew it would be an earth-shattering declaration. It would open up a world of trouble leading directly back toward Eric Duncan. She'd vowed to never allow it to happen. It was all so very sad, Sage realized. So many people had been affected by the selfish actions of one woman whose desire for a baby had led her to do the unthinkable.

With a sinking sensation, Sage realized there was no reason to stay in Alaska much longer. She'd already met her biological family and found proof in the form of the photo in Piper's diner that showed her mother had been in Owl Creek twenty-five years ago. If she hung around for a few more weeks it would only serve to complicate matters.

Sage released a belabored sigh. She was already becoming enmeshed in the fabric of daily life in this close-knit town and she cared deeply about so many people here. She had come to Alaska seeking answers and along the way she'd discovered so much about her roots, the North family and the Alaskan way of life. God had been with her every step of the way, giving her the strength and purpose to dig into her past. There would forever be a hole that couldn't be filled up by anything but her birth family, but she felt grateful for all the experiences and the knowledge she'd gained.

All she could hope for in this situation was the grace to walk away knowing she'd done her best in an impossible predicament.

*Thank you, Lord, for allowing me to go on this journey. And for bringing so many wonderful people into my life.*

Hank's handsome face flashed before her eyes. She couldn't stop thinking about him or the kiss they'd shared. It had taken her a long time to admit it to herself, but she had powerful feelings for Hank, ones she'd never felt before in her life. Saying goodbye to him would be extremely difficult.

Blinking back tears, Sage couldn't imagine how she'd ever thought this journey could ever bring her closure.

She would be full of regret for the rest of her life about the road not traveled. Life wasn't fair! She had come all this way only to have her heart wrapped up in a man she could never have. In truth, she didn't want to head back to Florida with the knowledge that she'd never be able to fully explore her tender feelings for Hank.

There were many dangling questions. What might have developed with Hank if she'd told the Norths the truth and stayed here in Owl Creek? What ties might she have been able to forge with her family members if given the time? She really didn't have a choice in the matter. The circumstances were completely out of her control. Jane Duncan had set this terrible situation in motion all those years ago and now she had been left holding the bag. Keeping silent was the only way to ensure that the man who'd raised her and always loved her remained safe.

Although her heart felt heavy at the moment, Sage didn't regret coming all this way to Alaska because this trip had forever changed her. Her heart was now permanently engraved with all the people in Owl Creek who'd touched her life in one way or another.

## Chapter Eleven

When she woke up the next morning, Sage knew she had to tell Trudy she was leaving Owl Creek earlier than expected. The innkeeper had been so gracious and kind to her during her stay and it made her ache a little inside to even think about saying goodbye to her. But it was something she knew she had to do.

Sage had tossed and turned throughout the night as her conscience poked and prodded her. Kissing Hank had shown her that she'd become overly invested in him and the entire town. It was time to go back to her life in Florida, even though she knew she'd be leaving a piece of her heart right here in Alaska.

At the moment, Owl Creek was in the middle of a major snowstorm. Trudy seemed very nonchalant about the whirling snow and heavy winds, having seen this type of weather system many times before in the past. Sage had never seen anything like it in her life and she worried about Hank keeping safe in the storm since Trudy had made a point to tell her he'd gone into the sheriff's office as usual this morning.

"Let's sit down for a cup of tea, shall we?" Trudy suggested. "Addie is napping, so my hands are free for a bit. It won't be as good as the tea Iris serves over at Tea Time, but it will still hit the spot."

"Of course it will. Let me get the teacups and saucers from the cupboard."

Sage began taking out the tea set while Trudy busied herself at the stove. Within minutes they were seated at the kitchen table, sipping peach tea and nibbling on shortbread cookies. It felt nice to be having a leisurely afternoon tea while the storm raged on outside.

After taking a sip of the fragrant brew, Sage placed the cup down on the saucer and cleared her throat. "Trudy, there's something I wanted to talk to you about."

Trudy looked at her and smiled. Her eyes twinkled. "Let me guess. Is this about Hank? I saw the two of you getting along beautifully last night." She winked at her. "In case you're wondering, I fully approve."

She shook her head. "No, it's not about Hank. We're just friends, by the way." The moment she uttered the words, her heart rejected them as false. *Did friends kiss in the moonlight?* she wondered. Not that she would disclose that tidbit to Trudy under any circumstances. If she did, his mother might just start planning their wedding. Why did the thought of spending forever with Hank seem so appealing?

"Well, you could have fooled me," Trudy said, making a face. For the first time since Sage had known her, the innkeeper looked slightly grumpy.

Sage broke eye contact with Trudy. She couldn't bear to look in her eyes and see disappointment. "I've decided to cut my visit to Owl Creek short. I'm going to be making plans to head home early next week."

Trudy let out a shocked sound, causing Sage to look over at her.

"Oh no, Sage! Did something happen? I thought you were enjoying your time here."

"Oh, I am, Trudy," she said, reaching out to hold her hand. "It's been a wonderful sojourn. I just think I should be with my father right now. He's dealing with a mountain of grief and he shouldn't have to ride this out alone."

"I understand, Sage. Truly I do. I can't say I'm not bitterly disappointed though. I'm going to miss you something fierce, and I daresay many others will feel the same way." She stared pointedly at Sage. It was obvious she was making a reference to Hank, but Sage wasn't going to go down that road with Trudy. She'd made her peace the other night with the fact that she and Hank wouldn't lead to anything but a dead end. She needed to be realistic.

"You've become an honorary daughter to me. I couldn't ask for a better lodger." Trudy wiped away a tear from her cheek. "Look at me getting all sentimental."

"Trudy, you've been a godsend to me during this really difficult period in my life. I'll always be grateful for your friendship and hospitality." Sage found herself getting choked up too. Goodbyes were never easy for her.

"I hope you won't be a stranger to us here in Owl Creek. I'd love for you to come back for another visit, and I promise to write to you and send pictures of

Addie. These little ones change so much in the blink of an eye."

Sage knew in all likelihood she wouldn't be returning to this quaint Alaskan town. It would be like reopening a wound. Leaving once without telling the Norths the truth would be painful enough, but she couldn't bear to come back for a visit, only to leave again. And although it would be sweet to receive pictures of Addie it would only serve to remind her of everything she could never have with Hank.

Why lead Trudy on and make her think it might happen? Sage simply smiled and nodded.

Trudy continued talking. "Will you promise to stay for the cook-off competition? It's coming up on the weekend. I could really use another set of hands on my team." Trudy crossed her hands in prayer-like fashion. "Please please please stay for it," she begged.

The Owl Creek cook-off competition had been something Sage had been eagerly anticipating. She wouldn't miss it for the world. It would be her last event in town before she said her final goodbyes in a few days.

"Of course I will," Sage agreed. "Are you still planning to make chili? That's a personal favorite of mine."

Trudy clapped her hands together. "That's the plan. And I'm calling it Trudy's knock-your-socks-off chili. Only a few people know my secret ingredients." She leaned in toward Sage and said, "I add honey and a few pieces of North Star chocolate." She placed a finger at her lips. "Don't tell anyone. People have been asking me for years."

Sage threw back her head and chuckled. "Your secret is safe with me," she assured her.

Never in her life had she heard of anyone adding chocolate to chili. All roads really did lead to chocolate in Owl Creek.

Trudy winked at her. "Laugh all you want. I'm fixing to win that cook-off with my chili and earn some major bragging rights."

Sage smirked. "You might have some serious competition. From what I hear, Hank is making something special himself."

"Do me a favor, will you?" Trudy asked. "Make sure you let Hank know you'll be leaving town soon."

Sage frowned. "Of course. Why is it so important to you?"

The older woman fiddled with her fingers, twisting them around and around. "I know you said you're just friends, but Hank has suffered a lot of losses in his life. I don't want him to feel blindsided by the news. I'll let you tell him in your own time. Just don't wait too long."

"I won't," Sage promised, taking a long sip of her tea. The thought of saying goodbye to the people she'd gotten close to caused a groundswell of panic to hit her. Perhaps she'd wait until the day of the cook-off to tell everyone else the news. They would probably be so engaged by the event that they wouldn't even process her news. Which would be best because, all things considered, she preferred to depart Owl Creek as quietly as she'd arrived in the Alaskan hamlet.

The back kitchen door suddenly burst open, causing Sage to let out a little scream. Trudy stood up from her chair in a defensive posture. Relief flooded through

Sage at the realization that it was Hank standing there.
He was leaning against the doorjamb covered in a liberal
coating of freshly fallen snow, looking for all intents
and purposes like the abominable snowman.

Hank stood at the back door to his mother's house
feeling like a human icicle. He couldn't remember a
time when he'd felt so frozen to the bone. On his way
to Trudy's house his truck had broken down. And to
make matters worse, his cell phone had died, leaving
him stranded without a ride or a means of communi-
cation. Due to the storm, no other vehicles were on
the road to rescue him. He had been up a creek without a paddle.

"Hank! Come in from the cold!" Trudy urged,
quickly making her way to his side.

"Don't mind if I do," he said, wincing as he walked
in. "I'm sorry for bringing snow in, Mama, but my feet
might be frostbitten."

"What happened, Hank?" Sage asked. "Did you
walk from town?"

He nodded, his teeth chattering. "Sadly, my truck
broke down about three miles or so down the road.
There were no houses on the route where I could seek
shelter, so I had to hoof it here."

Sage let out a gasp of disbelief. "You must be frozen all the way through!"

"Help him get that jacket off, will you, Sage?" Trudy
asked. Sage didn't waste any time helping. He felt ener-
gized simply by her close proximity to him, and when
she brushed against him as she took his coat off, he
caught a whiff of a honey scent.

Hank shivered. He was frozen to the bone and in need of some sustenance. All during his three-mile walk he'd dreamed about a mug of piping hot tea and his mama's home-baked bread. He could hear his stomach grumbling.

"Hank. Go inside the spare room and I'll bring you a pair of sweatpants, socks and Jack's old robe. You need to get out of those wet clothes," Trudy commanded in a no-nonsense voice. Hank followed her instructions, hobbling down the hallway after struggling out of his boots.

Switching up his clothes made him feel refreshed. He returned to the kitchen while Trudy went to the laundry room with his wet garments.

"Sit down. I'll get you a cup of tea. Are you hungry?" Sage asked. He nodded, feeling too depleted of energy to answer. Folks who weren't used to Alaskan weather didn't understand how things could turn deadly in a heartbeat. If he'd stayed out in the elements much longer he might be dealing with the long-term consequences of frostbite.

He watched Sage as she foraged in the cupboard for cups, then turned the kettle on. Her movements were graceful and efficient. Within minutes he had a cup of tea placed in front of him along with a serving of cheesy toast. Hank didn't waste any time digging in. He hadn't eaten since early this morning.

"Feeling better?" Sage had a smile on her face as she looked at his empty plate. Not even a crumb remained. He'd also drained his teacup.

Hank leaned back in his seat. "Yes. Thank you. It's

funny how quickly the tables can turn. I'm usually the one keeping watch over everyone else in town."

"Now it's your turn to be taken care of, Sheriff. I imagine you've earned it."

He fiddled with the handle of his teacup, his gaze focused on it. "When I was out there in the snow I kept thinking about Addie. I kept praying for God to watch over her in the event that something happened to me."

"Oh, Hank…" Sage murmured. "I'm so sorry your thoughts took you to that place."

"I suppose it's the product of being Addie's only parent. It's one of my greatest fears. If something happens to me, she'll be parentless."

"That's not going to happen!" Sage said in a scolding tone. "And if it does, you have Trudy and Piper as wonderful stand-ins, not to mention her honorary uncles, Gabriel and Connor. It's nice to have a village."

"That's true. None of them would ever let me down, or Addie. You haven't met Connor yet, have you?"

"No, I haven't had the pleasure. Maybe at the cookoff we'll run into each other."

"I'll make a point to introduce you unless Beulah beats me to it. She's a very proud grandmother."

"Knowing Beulah, that's not hard to imagine," Sage said, her expression inscrutable. Sometimes Hank wished he could get inside her head and see exactly what she was thinking. There still remained a little mystery about her, which both perplexed and fascinated him. With every moment he spent in her presence, Hank found himself wanting to know every single thing about her.

The sound of Addie's chattering reverberated from

the baby monitor. He made a move to get up from his chair, only to be stopped by Sage.

"I'll go get her, Hank. Please don't get up," Sage insisted, placing her hand on his arm.

She returned a short while later with Addie nestled against her chest. His daughter looked very content, which wasn't always the case with people outside the family. But because she saw Sage each and every day, they'd developed a close bond. Hank couldn't resist reaching for Addie. It had been a long day without seeing his little girl.

"Hank, I told Trudy the news earlier. I'm going home in a few days."

Hank felt his heart lurch at Sage's unexpected announcement. Although he'd known she would be leaving town before too long, he hadn't imagined it happening so soon. The knowledge left him feeling deflated. He'd just begun to explore his feelings for her and now she would soon be nothing more than a memory.

"I'm sorry to hear it. You've been a fine addition to this town." His throat felt clogged.

For the life of him he couldn't think of anything else to say, but he knew he wanted to come up with something to make her change her mind and stay.

Addie leaned her body away from him, stretching out her arms in Sage's direction. She let out a high-pitched squeal. Sage smiled at Addie and took her in her arms. She pressed a kiss by her temple. "I'm going to miss you so much, Addie. I'll never forget you," she whispered near her ear.

Although he didn't say it, Hank would miss Sage

just as much. And he wouldn't ever forget her. Forgetting Sage would be like trying to forget the magnificent northern lights. It just wasn't possible.

A few minutes later, Trudy returned along with Piper, who was still in her pajamas.

"What happened to you?" Piper asked Hank.

"My truck broke down. Long story short, I had to walk from the Beckworths' Farm all the way here."

His sister let out a low whistle. "Yikes! I slept through the whole thing. It was snowing so hard this morning I didn't even bother opening up the diner. Can I get you anything, Hank?"

"No, I'm good. A few more minutes out there and I think I might have been dealing with frostbite. Between Mama and Sage I've been pretty spoiled," he said. Piper wiggled her eyebrows at him when Sage wasn't looking. He didn't even bother telling her she'd gotten things wrong. He had the feeling he was wearing his feelings for Sage like a neon sign.

"Hey, Piper, can I borrow some snow pants?" Sage asked.

"Sure thing," she said. "Are you going out there in all that snow?"

Sage's grin was infectious. "Yes! I'm from Florida. This type of snow event is as likely as a volcano erupting. I'm going to seize the moment and head outside. I might never get an opportunity like this again."

Piper left the kitchen, quickly returning with a pair of pink snow pants. In a flash Sage had put them on along with her winter boots, hat and gloves.

Once she went outside Hank peered through the window, watching as she twirled around in the snow, then lifted her face toward the sky as snowflakes landed on her. She jumped up and did a cartwheel in the snow, her legs knee-deep in the fluffy white stuff. When she began doing a playful little dance, Hank let out a bark of delight. Piper began to giggle while Trudy couldn't keep a straight face even though she tried at first. When Sage looked toward the window and spotted them watching her, she playfully stuck out her tongue. Next thing he knew she was on her back in the snow flapping her arms around. It made him smile. She was a big kid at heart, he realized. Her joy was contagious.

"Isn't she silly?" he asked Addie, who placed her hands against the glass and lightly banged on it. It drew Sage's attention. She picked up a mound of snow and threw it toward the window where it landed with a splat. Addie descended into a fit of the giggles. Hank loved the tinkling sound of his daughter's laughter. It made him feel as if all was wonderful in her world.

This was what he wanted for himself and Addie. Someone who saw the simple pleasures in life and didn't hesitate to embrace them with gusto. This was what was missing in his world. He'd been so insistent on staying away from any female who might tempt him to feel again, but in the process he had shortchanged himself and Addie. One of these days he would have to tell his mother she'd been right about him and the issues he had been holding on to from the past.

Wonderful things happened when you acted on simple faith. He might not have a future with Sage, but she'd taught him that his heart wasn't as closed off as he'd believed. And maybe, if he could summon the courage, he might ask her to stay in Owl Creek.

# Chapter Twelve

The delicious smell of food hung in the air outside the Snowy Owl Diner. A large tent had been set up where the contestants were all gathered to present their culinary dishes. Even though it was a small-town event, people had come from far and wide to try to win the substantial monetary prize. Sage's focus was on helping Trudy with her savory chili dish. After tasting it during the prep stage, she was convinced Trudy had a decent shot at the trophy, although she predicted Piper was going to give her a run for her money. Even Hank might have a surprise or two up his sleeve with his famous corn bread.

Sage was trying to stay upbeat despite the fact that she was already having withdrawal symptoms. The pace of life here in Owl Creek suited her. Alaska was so different from anything she'd ever experienced, which left her craving more of it. She'd acclimated to the weather and the shorter hours of daylight. She was really proud of her ability to drive on snow-covered Owl

Creek roads. She'd even driven home from town the other day through fog as thick as pea soup.

Her goal was to allow herself an enjoyable last event in Owl Creek before she departed for home. Trudy had made up long-sleeved T-shirts for the two of them to wear bearing the slogan Team Trudy. Wearing it made Sage feel as if she was a part of something special. Right before the judges began walking around to taste test the offerings, Sage said to her, "You've got this!" She held up her hand in the air for a high five which Trudy gladly provided.

Out of the corner of her eye she saw someone waving in her direction. It was Hank. His table was located a few tables down. Gabriel and Connor were standing with him and they were all wearing black T-shirts with the words The Three Amigos printed on them. Sage made a gesture toward the shirts and gave him a thumbs-up.

She spotted Piper setting up her table and she made a beeline to her. Piper had been up and out of the inn well before Sage had arisen this morning. She had no idea what Team Piper had whipped up for the contest, but she knew it would be delectable.

"Hey, Piper. I just wanted to wish you well today," she said.

"Thanks, friend. I'm so happy you're helping Mama out today. I know it means a lot to her."

"I was pretty happy she asked me. It makes me feel like a part of Owl Creek."

Piper stumbled as she placed a pan down on the table. She muttered a few angry words, then lightly kicked the table's leg. "If one more thing goes wrong I'm going back to bed!" she said with a snarl.

"Are you all right? You seem super stressed out." Sage remarked, placing her hand on her friend's shoulder. She seemed as if she was about to crack wide open.

"I'm hanging in there. I'm just feeling a bit under pressure at the moment."

"Because of the cook-off? You don't need to feel nervous. From what I can see, it's all good fun."

Piper's lips trembled. "It's not the cook-off, Sage. I only entered because it's tradition…and I need the money for the diner. Things have been really slow lately and I'm getting worried about its long-term future."

Sage put her arm around the other woman. "Things will most likely get better after winter when tourism picks up. Can you ask Trudy or Hank for any financial help? I'd help you myself if I could afford to."

"That's sweet of you, Sage, but I could never accept it. Mom and Hank have already done so much to support my dream. I can't really ask them to do much more."

Sage sighed. "I wish there was something I could do to help. I don't like this look of dread on your face."

"Just listening helps. The diner means so much to me. It was my dad's pride and joy. I don't want to disappoint him."

"I know carrying on his legacy is important to you. And from where I'm standing, you're doing a wonderful job."

"Now you're going to make me cry, Sage," Piper said, reaching out and embracing her.

It seemed that everywhere she turned, God was highlighting the importance of relationships between fathers and their daughters. Piper and Jack. Hank and Addie. And her own loving relationship with her own father.

As she walked back toward her table, Sage couldn't help but feel a bit forlorn about not being able to stick around to help Piper. She was honored that her friend had confided in her about her money woes. If only she could find a way to solve her problem with the diner.

As she walked past Hank's table he waved her over. She couldn't help but smile at the T-shirts. It must be nice to have a kinship like the one Hank, Gabriel and Connor shared. Although she had friends back in Coral Gables, she'd never had close connections like these men shared. Once again she wondered if her life would have been vastly different growing up here in Owl Creek. Maybe she and Piper would have been best friends.

"Everything okay with Piper? She seems a little quiet. But maybe she's just afraid she's about to lose to the three amigos." Hank jokingly puffed out his chest, earning himself a smile from Sage.

"She's got a lot on her mind," she said, knowing it wouldn't be right to violate Piper's trust. It wasn't her place to tell Hank about his sister's troubles. Trudy, Hank and Piper were a tight-knit family who clearly adored one another. She prayed Piper would reach out to her family and ask for their assistance. Carrying such a weight on her shoulders would surely drag her down if things didn't get better at the diner.

She made a face at Hank. "And I seriously don't

think she's scared of your famous corn bread." She held up her fingers and did the sign for air quotes when she uttered the word famous. "Whatever she has under that aluminum foil smelled pretty delectable. I imagine she's going to have you shaking in those boots of yours."

Hank grinned. "So you've got jokes about my corn bread, huh." He leaned in so his face was close to her own. "I'm going to do something that might be against the rules, but I'm going to make an exception since you're an out-of-towner." He reached into one of his covered pans and pulled out a piece of corn bread. "Go on and try it."

Sage let out a sigh. "I'm not a really big fan of the stuff, to be honest."

"You're going to love mine. It's Alaskan sourdough corn bread."

Knowing Hank wasn't going to stop asking her, Sage tentatively took a bite. When the flavor hit her tongue, she closed her eyes and let out a sigh of satisfaction. When she opened her eyes, he was looking at her with an expectant expression stamped on his face.

"This is…incredible!" She took another bite, then ended up pushing all of it in her mouth.

"See," Hank crowed, rocking back on his heels and smiling like a Cheshire cat. "I don't want to say I told you so, but I did tell you my corn bread was legendary."

Sage covered her mouth with her hand until she finished swallowing. "I won't argue with you on that one. Well done, Sheriff!"

"Hey there!" Connor walked over and stuck out his hand. "I'm Connor North. I've heard a lot about you,

Sage Duncan." Sage shook hands with him, swallowing past her nervousness.

Hank tried to discreetly jab him in the side, then rolled his eyes in his direction.

"Have you?" she asked, darting a glance at Hank, who looked extremely sheepish.

"Yes," Connor answered, shooting his friend an annoyed look. "From my grandmother. She's a card-carrying member of your fan club."

"Well, the feeling is completely mutual. I love Beulah and her generous heart," Sage said, feeling slightly unnerved by being so near to her brother. Up close, Connor was even more handsome than she'd previously realized. With his dark hair and striking blue eyes, he exuded a familiar air. Sage realized there was something about him that reminded her of herself. It made her nervous, wondering if anyone else might pick up on it.

Connor looked around the immediate area. "She's coming today, but I haven't seen her yet. I have a feeling she'll be stopping by your table."

"I'll look for her," she said, grinning at the thought of getting to spend more time with Beulah. "It was nice to meet you, Connor. I better head back to Trudy." With a wave, she said her goodbyes and walked away. Meeting Connor completed the circle. With the exception of Braden North, who wasn't currently residing in Owl Creek, she'd met her entire family.

Connor was a larger-than-life human being in her eyes. From everything Hank had told her about him, he was a good person. Strangely enough, she felt a burst of pride knowing he was her sibling.

"Did I see you over there sampling the competition?" Trudy asked, frowning.

Within seconds she was laughing, unable to keep up the pretense of being upset with Sage.

Sage stared at Hank's mama for a few moments, trying to take a mental snapshot of this beautiful, nurturing woman. In the weeks and months to follow Sage would cherish all of her special moments with Trudy.

"The judges are beginning to make their rounds," Trudy called out to Sage. "Let's get in position."

Nodding, she took her place next to Trudy and began to ladle chili from the huge pots on the burner.

After only a few minutes, Sage wiped her hand across her brow. Serving up the chili and standing by a heater was making her work up a sweat. She rolled up her sleeves and began to fan herself with her hand. She'd never imagined the inside of the outdoor tent would be so hot. As the judges stepped up to the table, Trudy and Sage began to line up the bowls side by side. It had been Sage's idea to offer a piece of savory bread to dunk into the chili.

One by one the judges came through, sampling the dish and writing a score down on a piece of paper. Willa came forward and reached for a bowl of chili. Sage handed it to her with a smile. She hadn't known Willa was one of the judges. Willa greeted them with a nod and a huge smile. Sage felt a burst of happiness just knowing she was part of something bigger than herself. It was amazing to feel as though she was a member of this tight-knit community.

While the judges convened to make their decisions, Sage stood with Trudy and tried not to get distracted by Hank, who was goofing around with Connor and Gabriel. When an announcement was made to gather around so the judges could declare the winner, everyone made their way toward the stage. Trudy reached out and grabbed ahold of Sage's hand.

Willa stepped up to the microphone. "It's my pleasure to announce that the winners of the tenth annual cook-off are... Trudy Miller and Sage Duncan," she said in a triumphant voice. Trudy began jumping up and down with excitement. Sage was swept up in the celebratory mood of the crowd as everyone cheered and congratulated them. It was sheer pandemonium.

Hank suddenly appeared at her side, his face lit up with a grin. He leaned toward her and pressed a kiss on her cheek. "Congratulations!" he said. "Now that you've won the cook-off competition, you can't possibly leave town." He reached for her hand and squeezed it. A feeling of warmth spread through her at his touch.

"I didn't really do anything. Trudy did all the heavy lifting," Sage replied with a self-conscious laugh, thinking he was teasing her about remaining in town. But when she locked gazes with Hank she saw truth radiating from his eyes. He wasn't joking in the slightest!

"In my humble opinion, this town could greatly benefit by having someone like you as a resident. I like spending time with you, Sage. And I really do wish you would stay a while longer here in Owl Creek."

She looked up at him and smiled. His sweet words caused goose bumps to prickle on the back on her neck.

The way Hank made her feel was unlike anything she'd ever experienced before. It was crazy, but he was actually causing her to reconsider leaving Owl Creek.

He was making her believe that with him by her side, perhaps everything might be all right if she stayed. It was what she'd been looking for her entire life without even knowing it. A soft place to fall.

Was there a way to stay here in town a bit longer? Could she allow herself to further explore her feelings for Hank? Even though she'd been convinced that leaving was her only option, the handsome sheriff was forcing her to rethink her plans.

Hank looked outside the kitchen window as Sage and Addie frolicked in the snow. Sage had insisted on celebrating the cook-off win by spending quality time with Addie outside. He could feel a gigantic grin overtaking his face. For a girl from Florida, Sage really seemed to be enjoying the frosty Alaskan temperatures here in Owl Creek. She'd acclimated perfectly. Before going outdoors with Addie, she'd assured him that she didn't plan to stay outside for long. Sage knew Addie was too little to be exposed to cold temperatures for extended periods of time. It was sweet how painstakingly Sage had bundled Addie up in a snowsuit so she wouldn't suffer from the elements.

Hank had gotten used to Sage's presence in his life. He'd already decided to try to convince her to stay in Owl Creek for a longer period of time. He couldn't ignore the powerful way he felt when they were together. His heart was urging him to fight for this beautiful woman.

"Hank, can you give me a hand with these linens? My back is already aching something fierce." Trudy's voice intruded on his thoughts.

Hank glanced in her direction. She had a look of

pain etched on her face. He could tell with just one glance that her rheumatoid arthritis was flaring up again. Guilt trickled through him. He'd been so busy gazing at Sage that he'd missed the opportunity to step in earlier to help her out.

He swiftly made his way to her side. "Of course, Mama. You should have just asked me in the first place." Hank reached over and lifted up the laundry bin. "What have I told you about overextending yourself? You don't want to put your back out again. You were laid up for weeks last time."

Trudy let out a groan. "I most certainly don't, but these linens need to be cleaned. After all, I am running a bed-and-breakfast." She winked at her son. "Thankfully the washing machine will take care of the hard part."

He chuckled. His mother was incredibly hardworking and she never surrendered, despite some health issues she'd endured.

Hank began walking toward the laundry room when his feet got tripped up in a piece of laundry on the floor. He bent down and picked it up, his entire body stiffening. Suddenly, his stomach lurched. It was a blanket adorned with owls. He felt the fabric between his fingers. It looked fairly old and a sickening knowledge washed over him. He'd seen this blanket before, courtesy of Nate and Willa who had provided photos of it. It was part of the evidence in the Lily North file.

He held up the blanket. "Where did this come from?" He couldn't hide the anguish in his tone.

His mother's brows furrowed. "What's wrong, Hank? You don't look so good."

"Tell me, Mama. Please. It's important." He found himself holding his breath awaiting her response. It felt as if his entire future was hanging in the balance.

Trudy shrugged. "These came from Sage's room and my own. I haven't stripped the beds in the other rooms yet. Why do you ask?"

Hank didn't know what to tell his mother. She would be floored by the idea that Sage was nothing more than a con artist. Anger rose up inside him at the thought of his mother being so betrayed by someone she'd treated with infinite kindness. This time they'd *all* been burned.

The back door flew open, bringing with it a strong gust of wind. Sage was laughing as she jiggled Addie in her arms. Hank watched with his heart in his throat as she leaned toward his daughter and nuzzled noses with her. How many times had he prayed for a woman to come into his life who would share a bond with his baby girl? How many nights had he gotten on his knees and asked the Lord to allow him to move past Theresa's betrayal? And just when he thought he'd turned a corner, he'd made a life-altering discovery that had nearly brought him to his knees.

"Mama. Take Addie, please, and go upstairs." His words sounded commanding, brooking no argument. Trudy looked back and forth between him and Sage, then walked over and plucked his baby girl from Sage's arms. She quickly left the kitchen, her features pinched and strained.

Sage's brows were knitted together. "Did I do something wrong?" she asked. It was shocking to see the look of bewilderment etched on her face. Did she not have a conscience?

Hank slowly walked toward her, holding out the blanket as he got within a few feet of her. "This turned up in the laundry Mama collected from your room. Can you tell me why you have it among your things?"

Sage's eyes went wide. Her lips began to tremble. He could almost see the wheels turning in her head as she tried to process that she'd been found out.

"Hank, I can explain," she said in a halting voice.

"Can you? I highly doubt it. There are only two plausible reasons you would have this in your possession. One is that you're Lily North and the other is that you were using the blanket so you could pretend to be her. Either way, you've been lying ever since you came to town."

A wounded look passed over her face. "I'm not Theresa, Hank. I didn't come to Alaska to scam the North family."

He sucked in a steadying breath. "So, you're telling me you're actually Lily?"

She slowly nodded her head. Sadly, Hank didn't know what to think. He'd been scammed before by his ex, a woman who had ruthlessly tried to deceive the entire town. He was well aware of how conniving people could be when they wanted to work their own agendas. At the moment he couldn't believe a single thing Sage was telling him, even though he wanted to trust her at her word.

"Maybe you're confused about what the right thing to do is, but I'm not." Hank reached for his coat hanging on the back of a kitchen chair. He shot Sage a pointed look as he put it on. "We're heading over to the Norths' home. If you're really Lily, I think they've waited long enough to hear that you're alive and well.

"And if you're not really her, they have a right to know that, as well."

Sage sat next to Hank in the passenger seat nervously fidgeting with her fingers as they headed to the Norths' home.

*She'd lost him.* Not that Hank had ever been hers in the first place, but it hurt to see the look of disgust stamped on his face. It was strange how certain things became crystal clear in moments of crisis. Sage now knew she was in love with Hank. It had been happening gradually over the last few weeks, but now he was firmly cemented in her heart. She'd never imagined falling for someone in such a short time, but there was no question in her mind that she had fallen head over heels for the good-hearted sheriff.

But it was all ruined now because of her withholding the truth from him. Hank was a man who lived by a code of honor. Truth. There were no shades of gray with him.

The ride passed in silence as tension simmered in the air between them. Hank didn't spare her a single glance. When they reached the Norths' residence, Hank pulled the passenger-side door open for her, his face grim as they made eye contact. She wanted so badly to apologize to him again, but she had the feeling he didn't want to hear a single word she had to say. Sage couldn't blame him. For all intents and purposes, she seemed like a colossal liar. A *fraud*.

A carbon copy of his deceitful ex-girlfriend.

Once they were standing at the front door, Sage began to shiver uncontrollably. The idea of facing her birth family felt overwhelming to her. Even though she knew the situation had been of her own making, she felt blindsided. Never in a million years had she imagined being found out by Hank this way. It had all blown up in her face.

She turned toward him. "I—I don't think I can do this."

Hank's lip curled. "You don't really have a choice." Sage took a step away from him.

She barely recognized him at the moment. He was radiating pure anger.

After Hank buzzed the door a few times, Willa opened it for them. There was a look of surprise on her face when she saw Sage at his side. "Hank! We've been anxiously awaiting your arrival since your call. I didn't know Sage would be here."

She had overheard Hank's phone call to Willa and Nate before they'd left the house. In a very abrupt tone he'd told them that he needed to talk to the family regarding a matter of utmost importance.

"Come on in! Don't be shy," Nate urged, appearing behind his wife in the doorway.

Hank made a motion with his hand, waving Sage inside before he stepped over the threshold behind her. His features were set in grim lines.

"Beulah, Jennings and Connor are joining us," Willa said, as she led them down the hall toward the living room.

Once they entered the room, Connor jumped to his feet. "What's going on, Hank? Are you here as town sheriff?"

"I suppose you could say this is official business," Hank said, a muscle ticking in his jaw.

"Sage, why don't you take a seat?" Beulah suggested, patting the seat next to her.

"No, thank you. I'd rather stand," Sage answered, feeling too nervous to move a muscle.

She looked down at the floor, unwilling to make eye contact with anyone in the room.

Hank cleared his throat. "There's something I need to show you." He reached into the canvas bag he was holding and pulled out the owl blanket.

Willa let out a gasp that echoed in the room. "Wh-where did you get that? That's Lily's blanket. I'd know it anywhere!" She moved toward Hank and grabbed the blanket from his hand, then pressed it close to her face to examine it. Then she let out a keening sound.

"It's Sage's blanket. She brought it with her to town. Only she can tell you why she has it among her belongings," Hank said, his voice sounding matter of fact. He was all business now and she barely recognized him as the kind, bighearted man she'd fallen for.

Nate moved to his wife's side, worry etched on his rugged features. "What is it, Willa?"

"Mom! What's going on?" Connor asked, alarm ringing out in his voice.

Willa pointed at the hem of the blanket, then swung her gaze in Sage's direction. "She's Lily, Nate. She's our little girl."

Nate's expression was pained. "We've been down this road before, sweetheart. It's just another scam from someone looking to exploit our family's tragedy." He shook his head as if in disbelief at the turn of events.

"Exactly!" Connor said, glaring in her direction. "She's just another con artist."

Willa shook her head, appearing dazed. "No, she's not. I stitched her initials on the hem of the blanket, right under the owl's wing. It's right here," she said, running her fingers over the stitchwork.

"No, Willa. It can't be true," Nate said, pain ringing out in his tone.

Willa tugged on his arm. "Don't you see it? She's our girl. They share the same hair color. Her eyes are brown. The jut of her chin is like mine. I can't believe we didn't see it before now." She turned back to look at Sage, her eyes begging for mercy. "Please. Tell us the truth. Are you Lily? Are you our daughter?"

Hank let out a shocked sound. Clearly, he hadn't seen this coming. He must have believed she was nothing more than an opportunist, and from the look on his face he appeared as stunned as she felt. And honestly? Being exposed in this manner *was* shocking. She hadn't prepared herself for it, not in the slightest. Sage felt her legs threatening to give out on her. Her first instinct was to run, but that wouldn't solve anything. This was a moment of reckoning twenty-five years in the making.

There was simply no way out of this but to tell the truth.

Although she wasn't sure she could ever adequately explain why she hadn't divulged everything weeks ago, Sage slowly nodded her head, locking eyes with the woman who'd given birth to her.

"Yes. It's true. I've had this blanket ever since I was born. I didn't come to Owl Creek to trick you or exploit you for personal gain. I'm your daughter. I'm Lily."

Sage's words nearly caused his heart to stop beating. Surely he'd misheard her? The reaction from everyone in his midst proved him wrong. There were tears and a torrent of emotion. Sage was Lily North? He'd convinced himself she was just another con artist, but with Willa authenticating the owl blanket, reality was staring him straight in the face.

He looked over at Sage. As soon as their eyes locked he saw the truth shimmering in her eyes. It was all true!

Willa began crying and she reached out her arms to Sage, pulling her into an embrace.

She held on tightly and began to rock back and forth as if Sage was a small baby. Nate let out a cry of joy and wrapped his arms around both of them. A mystified-looking Connor had his arm around Beulah, who looked completely floored by the news. Shock hung in the air as well as a feeling of jubilation.

"This is the best news in the world!" Jennings said, placing a kiss on Sage's cheek. "I never thought we'd lay eyes on you again. I don't care why you didn't tell us before today. I'm just ecstatic that you're home."

"We need her to take a DNA test," Connor said, his expression full of skepticism.

"Hush, Connor," Beulah chided her grandson. "The blanket is proof."

"I don't mind taking one," Sage said. "It's a good way to make certain I'm who I believe I am."

As he watched the drama unfold, all Hank felt was

pure, molten anger. How had he let himself get bamboozled by another dishonest woman? She'd been lying to everyone ever since she stepped foot into town. And now she was acting as if butter wouldn't melt in her mouth. Why were the Norths accepting everything she said at face value? She'd lied to them all!

*God... Not again. Why are You putting me through this pain all over again? Am I destined to be blind to deception and betrayal?*

Hank felt like a prize fool. Once more the wool had been pulled over his eyes by someone he deeply cared for. Sage Duncan wasn't who she'd claimed to be. This whole time she had been playing him for an idiot. She was Lily North, the missing Owl Creek baby. He'd spent time with this woman and opened himself up to her, yet she'd been sitting on this explosive secret for weeks. Clearly, nothing between them had been genuine. He'd worn his heart on his sleeve and asked her to stay in town when in reality she'd had her own agenda this whole time.

"I think you need to deal with this as a family," Hank said, nodding in Connor's direction before he turned on his heel and strode out of the room, determined to get as far away from Sage as possible. Only she wasn't Sage, he reminded himself with a groan. Everything about her had been a lie from the moment she'd arrived here in town. Once he'd stepped outside, he heard her calling after him.

"Hank! Please, stop! Come back. I'd like to explain why I kept my identity a secret." Although she was imploring him to stick around, he wasn't in the mood to hear her out. If she'd been honest with him from the start, he would have listened and helped her approach the North family. Instead she'd continued with her charade until it had all backfired.

Hank kept walking until she tugged hard at his jacket, forcing him to come to a stop. He turned around and frowned at her. "I really don't want to hear it!"

"Please, listen to me. There's so much you don't know, Hank. So much I should have told you from the very beginning."

"There's really nothing you can say at this point that I want to hear. Why don't you go back inside, Sage? The Norths are waiting for you. They're so desperate to get their daughter back after all these years. I'm sure they won't blame you for all the weeks of lies and evasions. From what I saw, they're ready to welcome you back into the fold with open arms."

"I didn't mean to lie to anyone," she choked out. "It was complicated."

Hank let out a harsh laugh. "You've been telling lies this entire time. In my experience, the truth isn't that hard to own. Tell me this. How long have you known you were Lily? Surely you didn't just find out."

She bit her lip. "I've known for a few months, but I couldn't really be certain. I wasn't sure. That's why I came to Owl Creek. I was trying to figure it all out."

*Months!* His blood ran cold. He felt his heart icing over. Against his better instincts he'd opened himself up to Sage. He had told her all about his past hurts. He'd *trusted* her. And now the door to his heart was firmly shut again. "That first day on the ferry I told you Connor was my best friend. You knew there were close ties between myself and the Norths, which served your purposes, didn't it? Every question you asked me about the abduction and the North family was digging for information."

"No! That's not true. I didn't target you because you're town sheriff or due to your ties to my birth family." Her lower lip trembled, and she hitched in a breath. "I tried not to like you, Hank, because of those relationships. I made a point to keep my distance, but it seemed as if we were always being drawn together. A sheriff was the last person I wanted in my life."

He knew Sage was trying to reason with him, but it was near impossible to hear anything she was saying. His anger ran too deep. Her betrayal hurt too much. His mind raced with all the times they'd discussed Lily's abduction, as well as the investigation and the Norths' desperate desire to find their missing daughter. It made him sick to his stomach that she'd been sitting on the truth for such a long time. It seemed heartless.

"Bravo. You really fooled us all, didn't you? And you put your family through unnecessary pain."

Sage flinched. Her face turned a paler color. "I know it must seem like that, but you don't have the whole story, Hank. There's so much I want to explain."

He clenched his teeth. "You should have told me weeks ago. You had plenty of opportunities to come clean. The world offers us plenty of excuses to not tell the truth. You knew what the Norths went through and what this town endured. Did I ever tell you that Piper's father was a suspect in the kidnapping? He went through torment to prove he was innocent. So the ripples from this case were widespread. The cuts run deep."

Her eyes went wide. "That's truly terrible."

"Well, I hope you get your happy ending with the Norths. They've waited a long time for this reunion."

"Come back inside with me," she said in a pleading tone. "I want you to be a part of it. I'm so very sorry." Sage sounded contrite and utterly broken. He faltered for a moment, unsure of himself. Wasn't forgiveness part of his faith? *Judge not, that ye be not judged.*

Just then he remembered Sage's plan to leave town. How could she have made that decision, knowing she'd be withholding the truth from the North family and the entire town of Owl Creek in the process? It caused his wrath to flare up again.

"No, thank you," he bit out. "It really has nothing to do with me. You've made that clear all along, haven't you?"

Sage seemed to be fighting back tears. She ducked her head down. Seeing her cry pained him. Growing up in a household of women had made him very susceptible to the slightest signs of weeping, but he clenched his teeth, trying not to be swayed by her waterworks. It was probably just one more manipulation. "I just want to ask one thing of you."

"You can ask me anything," she answered in a soft voice.

"Please don't hurt them. They're good people who only deserve happiness after all these years of suffering. They can't take much more."

"I wouldn't! I won't! I wasn't trying to hurt anyone. I just didn't know what to do or how to fix everything. I was in way over my head."

Hank scoffed. "Yeah. I know the feeling. So was I."

"Everything was real between us, Hank. *Please* don't lose sight of that."

He held up his hand as he walked away, letting her know in no uncertain terms he was done talking to her.

"Hank!" The sound of her voice crying out his name nearly brought him running back to her side. But he was on autopilot, trying desperately to move away from the gut-wrenching pain roiling in his body.

Hot tears stung his eyes. He couldn't remember the last time he'd cried. Perhaps on the day he'd discovered he was Addie's father. But those had been tears of joy not sorrow. These tears were forged from loss and devastation.

It was way more than being deceived. He was in love with Sage! The knowledge crashed over him like a tsunami. He'd fallen in love with her despite all his reservations and doubts. It had happened gradually, bit by bit, until now it was too late to take a step back. He'd done what he almost never did—he had stepped out on a ledge and allowed himself to free-fall, thinking he had a safety net to catch him. Instead, Hank had plummeted to earth and been given a healthy dose of reality.

## Chapter Thirteen

The last few days had been a whirlwind. There had been a celebratory mood amongst certain members of the North family as the news had sunk in about her true identity. Sage had submitted to a DNA test and the results were conclusive. She was Lily North! Willa and Nate had been overcome with joy, praising God for the reunion. Connor had been hesitant at first to fully believe her assertion that she was his long-lost sister. But he'd softened once Sage explained about the deathbed confession of the woman who'd raised her, as well as confided her fears for her father. He'd embraced her once the test results had come in.

They'd shed tears as a family and Nate had led them in prayer as they stood in a circle, tightly holding hands.

"Lord, we will be forever grateful to You for blessing us with Lily's return. Heavenly Father, thank You for listening to our fervent prayers to be reunited with our precious girl. You have answered our prayers and made our family whole again. Amen."

Beulah insisted on Sage staying at the family home so they could all exist under one roof as it should have been since the day she was born. Sage didn't have the heart to say no. Knowing she was providing such joy after such a long period of grief and sadness made her happy.

When she'd returned to the inn to collect her belongings, Trudy had been kind and a bit quieter than usual. She told Sage how delighted she was about her ties to the North family. Sage sensed there was a little bit of a wall between them due to Hank. She'd hurt Hank deeply, and knowing how much Trudy adored her son, Sage suspected there must be lingering feelings of anger toward her.

Sage didn't blame Trudy for being upset. Frankly, she was angry at herself. She should have found a way to tell Hank truth before it imploded on her. And it had been cruel to withhold the information from her birth family. Knowing what she knew now, things could have been handled in such a different manner. She had tried to handle the situation in the best way possible in order to protect her father, but it had all blown up in her face big-time.

Hank wanted nothing to do with her. And the worst part was he thought she'd been using him to get information about the North family, which was the furthest thing from the truth. In actuality she had tried to keep her distance from him ever since she'd discovered he was law enforcement. But her feelings for him hadn't allowed her to stay away from him for very long.

She loved Hank. It shocked her to her very core to realize she had fallen so deeply and completely in love with him in such a short time. When had he crept into her heart? All this time the feelings had been growing and growing until now her heart was full almost to overflowing. It didn't matter though. Not really. Hank would never allow himself to fall for a woman who'd withheld her identity and lied to his face.

When he'd told her all about his past with Theresa, Hank had revealed so much about himself and the manner in which she'd betrayed him. Sage's actions had caused him to relive that situation all over again. She wasn't sure she could forgive herself for hurting the man she loved. People always said truly loving a person meant you wanted the best for them, wishing them happiness even if it meant it wasn't with you. That's exactly what she felt for Hank.

The sound of footsteps alerted her to someone coming toward the living room. She blinked a few times at the sight of Eric Duncan standing a few feet away from her in the doorway. At six foot two, with salt-and-pepper-colored hair and a lean frame, he looked as distinguished as ever.

"Daddy!" Sage cried out. She ran toward him and threw herself against his chest.

"Sweetness!" Being cradled in her father's arms felt like a refuge. Everything in her world was so confusing right now, but she'd always been comforted by this man. He was solid and dependable. And loyal to a fault. Even though he wasn't her birth father, Sage would always consider him one of her two fathers. She was doubly blessed!

"What are you doing here? I can't believe you came all this way."

He reached for her hand and squeezed it. "Sweetheart, there's nothing I wouldn't do for you. The Norths called me a few days ago. They told me what happened and invited me to come stay for a bit." He swept his hand across her cheek. "I'm sure you already know it, but they're wonderful people. They said they thought you might need me. I hopped on the next available flight."

Sage knew her father didn't like to fly, so it was amazing that he'd dropped everything to support her. It was one of the many reasons she adored him.

"I almost thought you were a mirage. No one said a word. And I do need you. I feel like I've been whipped around by a tornado. I just want a small measure of peace now that everyone knows the truth."

"Why do you look so sad? It seems as if everything has been settled. The Norths assured me I'm not going to be prosecuted since we talked at length and they trust that I had nothing to do with the kidnapping. And you've been reunited with your birth family."

She squeezed her father's hand. "I know, Daddy. It's a real blessing. I'm so happy about it." Keeping her father safe had been her main goal this whole time. Her prayers had been answered.

He frowned at her. "What are you not telling me?"

Despite her intention to stay strong, she began to cry. She was pretty certain her huge sobs reverberated throughout the large family home. For so long she'd been hiding her feelings and her heartbreak. But now something had cracked wide open inside her and she could no longer hold back these emotions.

"There there," Eric soothed, patting her on her back.

"Tell me what's causing my darling girl to shed all these tears."

She spit out everything about meeting Hank on the ferry, developing a rapport with him and then being rejected by him when the truth about her identity came out.

"He's so angry at me, Daddy. He's made it clear he thinks I'm a big fat liar for withholding the truth. He doesn't want to have anything to do with me. It's breaking my heart."

He reached out and tilted her chin up so they were looking directly into each other's eyes. "Aaah. You're in love with him, Sage. I can see it shining in your eyes."

She nodded her head, unable to speak. If her father could see it so clearly, why couldn't Hank?

"It's the first time you've ever been in love." He scowled. "I'm not sure this Hank Crawford is worth all this heartache. If he's this unforgiving and intractable, perhaps he isn't the man for you."

"Daddy, you're wrong. Hank is the most amazing man I've ever known. The fault isn't with him. He lives by a code of honor and finds what I did unacceptable. He's been hurt in the past by lies and deception. I can't blame him for how he feels."

"You really have it bad, don't you?" he asked with a low chuckle. "In my experience, love isn't something any of us can afford to give up on."

"Love can't be one-sided." It hurt to acknowledge it, but at this moment all she had were her own strong feelings for Hank. Evidently, he didn't feel the same way.

"You're right about that, sweetness."

He held her in his arms for quite a long time, wiping

away her tears and whispering reassuring words to her. Suddenly she felt like the middle school version of herself who hadn't been invited to the homecoming dance.

When Sage finally moved out of his embrace, she looked up at him and spoke the words that had been weighing on her heart for months.

"Daddy, I really don't understand why she did it."

"If I'm being honest, neither do I," he admitted. "I've been thinking about it nonstop ever since you told me about her confession. Jane was desperate to have a baby. It just never happened for us. She couldn't conceive. For me, it wasn't the end of the world, but for your mother it was earth-shattering."

His jaw trembled with raw emotion. "We actually separated because of it. That's when she went on a trip with the youth group she'd joined through your aunt Cathy. I didn't even know where she went or any of the details since the group was out of state. When she came back she had you with her and she told me a story about a pair of underage teens who couldn't raise you and had abandoned you by a bridge. I'm ashamed to say I was so happy to be back with her and to have a new lease on our marriage with the baby of our dreams, I didn't ask many questions."

He bowed his head. "She had your birth certificate, which I know now was doctored. I should have pressed her for more answers. But in my defense, I never imagined you were stolen from another family. I truly thought we were saving an unwanted infant from a life of despair and neglect. We legally adopted you. Or so I thought at the time. With what I know now, I don't think the adoption was legal, Sage."

Her father was supplying her with a lot of information she'd never heard before. And it all added up with what Willa had told her once she'd seen a picture of Jane Duncan.

"I believe you," Sage told him. "She was clever in covering her tracks. Willa recognized her from the picture behind the counter at the Snowy Owl Diner. She said they opened up their home to many members of the youth group. She was one of the group leaders. It explains how she got access to the house. She used the alias of Emily Duncan while she was in Alaska. So when the FBI and the authorities were looking at the members of the youth group as suspects, they met up with a dead end. I hate to think she might have planned it in advance."

Sage shuddered. She got the chills every time she thought about being stolen in the middle of the night from her crib. Someday she would connect more of the dots, but for now she was content with what she'd discovered. And she knew it had given Nate and Willa a sense of closure to know what had happened and who was responsible.

He grimaced. "I talked to your aunt Cathy a few days ago and begged her for answers."

Sage's eyes widened. "And did your learn anything?"

"I did. Believe it or not, she's always known a lot more about your abduction than she's ever let on. It turns out your mother ran to Aunt Cathy's side in Maryland after she left Owl Creek with you. From what I gather, she stayed there for a few weeks hiding out. When Aunt Cathy pressed her about you, she confessed what she'd done and basically told her how she fled Alaska at night on the ferry and bundled you up in a little basket. At that time of night, the ferry was pretty empty, so there was no one who really noticed Jane." He cleared his throat, then went on. "Getting on a plane from Anchorage was simple. She paid off an attorney to help her falsify the paperwork."

Sage let out a shocked sound. "Why didn't Aunt Cathy report her to the authorities?"

"It's hard to say, but she was always protective of your mother. I think she was trying to spare her from spending the rest of her life in jail."

She shook her head, feeling disgusted. "While becoming her accomplice."

"I know it's hard to wrap your head around. Jane wasn't a woman of faith, but I'm convinced in her final days she accepted God as her Lord and Savior. It gives me a lot of comfort. She wasn't all bad even though she did a terrible thing."

Sage nodded. She had thought the same thing when she'd seen a Bible by her mother's bedside, but she hadn't allowed herself to hope that she'd accepted Christ before she had passed away. For most of her life she'd wondered why her mother hadn't been a believer. Knowing she might have discovered the Lord in her final days gave Sage a feeling of peace. "I think her confession was an attempt at redemption. She wanted to make things right. It doesn't excuse what she did, but it helps me know she wasn't completely lost."

"I agree, Sage," her father said with nod. "I pray for her every day. And you, as well as the entire North family. They've been through so much. I keep thinking of one of my favorite verses. *Weeping may endure for a night, but joy cometh in the morning.*"

"Amen to that," Sage whispered. "I don't know if they told you, but Willa and Nate want to hold a press conference tomorrow. It's their way of clearing up all the rumors flying around here in town. Everyone wants answers." She made a tutting sound. "I can't say I blame them. This has been an unsolved mystery for twenty-five years. Not to mention it will be like throwing a bone to the media outlets. Maybe then they'll give everyone some breathing room."

"You don't have to do it if you're not comfortable," Eric said thickly. "This may be a case of too much happening all at once. I worry you'll feel overwhelmed by it all."

Sage bit her lip. He was right. It did sound a bit daunting, but after all the secrets she had been harboring, she just wanted a bit of transparency.

"I think truth is important, but I'm not certain that I'm ready for a barrage of questions."

He nodded, worry etched on his craggy features. "I understand your concerns, Sage. And despite everything, I don't want the press to vilify your mother. But we can't sugarcoat the truth either. There's been enough of that, don't you think?" he asked.

Sage nodded. She had the feeling he regretted his own inability to confront his wife about the inconsistencies regarding the way Sage had come into their lives. He would probably always wonder about it and ask himself if he couldn't have done more to prevent it all.

She reached out and joined his hand with her own. "Let's face the future together as a united front. You,

me and my birth family. I honestly believe if we speak
from our hearts and a place of truth we can't lose. I
lost sight of that, Daddy, but I can promise you, I never
will again."

Hank couldn't remember a time in his life when
he'd felt so alone. Everyone and their brother was at
the press conference the North family had scheduled
to clear the air about their long-lost daughter. Even his
secretary, Dorinda, had left to make her way over to the
chocolate factory. The whole town of Owl Creek was
curious about the return of Lily North. Many wanted
answers they'd been waiting twenty-five years to hear.
He couldn't rightly blame them since the whole town
had been consumed by the mystery for decades.

The past few nights he'd tossed and turned as
thoughts of Sage tormented him. He couldn't get the
image of her crestfallen features, when he'd told her
off, out of his mind. Funny thing was he usually felt
relieved when he was able to speak his mind. But he
hadn't felt a bit of ease since the day of the cook-off.
Being at odds with Sage felt ten times worse than
what he'd experienced after his breakup with Theresa.
Which caused a light bulb to go off in his head. He
was genuinely in love with Sage in a way he'd never
experienced before.

The door to his office flew open without warning.
Piper stormed in, closely followed by his mother, who
was carrying Addie on her hip. Before he could com-
plain about them barging in without knocking, Piper
began talking in a raised voice.

"Hank, you have to listen to us. Mama has been trying to talk to you for days, but you're as stubborn as a mule. We love you. Your happiness means the world to us. Sage makes you smile. She's great with Addie. And from what I can see, she might even be in love with you. Not that you seem to have noticed or even care that she's hurting because of you."

"Piper! Take a breath," Trudy urged her daughter. She turned toward Hank. "By the way, I agree one hundred percent with everything your sister just said. You can't see what's so obvious to the rest of us. The two of you belong together!"

Hank leaned forward in his chair and placed his forearms on the desk. "What makes you think she loves me?" He hadn't considered his feelings might be reciprocated by Sage, even though he knew there was something powerful brewing between them. Pure adrenaline began racing through his veins.

"The only one who can answer that question is Sage," his mother snapped. "But since you're not talking to her, you might never find out." She placed Addie down on the floor. She began taking faltering steps toward her father. Every day her coordination was getting better.

"Way to go, baby girl! You're going to be running soon," he said, opening his arms wide.

Piper rolled her eyes. "Don't change the subject!" She tapped her watch. "The clock is ticking. I heard Sage might be going back to Florida soon. You need to make things right with her. *Now!*"

Piper and Trudy stared him down like he was the enemy. It had always been like this with his family. Two against one. What was the point in arguing with them? As with most things, they were right. He'd acted like a jerk. He hadn't allowed himself to see Sage's side of the situation at all. And he needed to talk to her before she left Owl Creek.

He let out a groan. "The two of you didn't have to march down here to confront me. I already know that I messed up with Sage. I've been racking my brain for a way to make amends with her. In case you were wondering, it's been killing me."

Piper sent him a satisfied look. "Happy to hear it," she said, folding her arms across her chest and tapping her foot.

"Piper, be nice," Trudy scolded.

"I was just kidding, Mom," Piper said. "Hank knows I want only the best for him."

Hank winked at her. "Ditto. Now give me some advice about how to approach Sage."

"She's over at the chocolate factory along with everyone else in town," Piper informed him. "I had to close the diner early since it was completely empty. Go to the press conference and tell her how you feel."

He ran a hand over his face. "I can't do that in front of everyone. How would that look, for the town sheriff to act like a lovesick fool?"

"You seriously need to get over yourself. Women love romantic gestures. It shows that you're willing to put your pride aside in order to get your happily-ever-after," Piper said.

Trudy vigorously bobbed her head up and down. "Listen to your sister. She's read hundreds of romance novels. She knows a lot about happy endings."

"Are you sure?" Hank asked, feeling a bit skeptical about showing up in front of the entire town. The very thought of all those prying eyes was enough to make him break out in hives.

"We're sure," Trudy and Piper said in unison.

Hank picked up Addie and handed her to Trudy. "Can you take her, Mama? I'm fixing to head over to the chocolate factory where I may or may not make an utter fool of myself."

Piper pounded him on the back. "Well, if you go down, at least it'll be in a blaze of glory. Your name will be on people's lips for weeks."

"That's very reassuring," Hank drawled.

"I'll see you later at the inn," Trudy said, bundling the baby up before she headed outside. "I can't keep Addie out in that cold, but I want a full report later." She pressed a kiss on her son's cheek. "Godspeed, Hank. Go get your happy ending, son."

Hank turned back toward Trudy and pulled her into a tight hug. "I'm sure going to try my best, Mama."

Standing on the steps of the chocolate factory in preparation for the press conference reminded Sage of the first time she'd come here with Hank, and her birth parents had been speaking to the press from this very spot. She had been under the impression that the press conference would be reduced to a few media outlets and a small number of residents. But now as she scanned the large crowd it caused butterflies to soar in her stomach. It appeared as if the entire town had turned out to hear about Lily North's mysterious return. She prayed everyone would understand her reasons for keeping silent during her stay in Owl Creek. It was time to lay everything out in the open.

Willa and Nate began by reading a statement about Sage's discovery of her true identity and her ties to Owl Creek. Although their words were emotional and eloquent, they didn't give any specifics about Jane Duncan. They had all agreed to handle it in a manner that would give Eric peace about his deceased wife. And even Connor concurred that seeking vengeance was pointless due to Jane's death. Aunt Cathy would be spared prosecution for aiding and abetting her sister.

"Mr. and Mrs. North. Will you be seeking charges against anyone with regard to the kidnapping of your daughter, Lily North?" a reporter asked.

Willa looked over at Nate before answering. "No, we will not. We are one-hundred-percent certain that the individual who abducted our daughter is no longer living. And we are also satisfied that her crime was carried out alone without assistance from anyone. Our wish is to move forward with the knowledge that our family is now whole. We'll leave the judgment up to God almighty."

Sage breathed a sigh of relief that they had all made the decision not to publicly name Jane Duncan as her abductor. She wasn't certain her mother deserved such grace, but she felt content with the outcome. It gave her a measure of peace.

A dark-haired female reporter threw out a question from the press area. "Hello. Grace Prescott reporting for the *Love, Alaska Gazette*. Sage. Lily. Which name are you going to use from now on? Do you have your own statement about your discovery?"

Sage stepped forward to speak into the microphone. "I plan to continue to use the name Sage since I've grown accustomed to it after all these years. In my heart I'll always cherish and honor my given name, Lily. My parents chose a beautiful name full of grace and beauty. I hope I've lived up to it." She took a deep breath, gathering her strength to speak. "I came to Owl Creek in search of answers, but I wasn't courageous enough to be completely open and honest with everyone. I just want to take this opportunity to apologize to anyone I may have hurt, including my family. You see, I wanted to protect the man who raised me from being implicated in the kidnapping. That man—Eric Duncan—never traveled to Alaska until recently. I just want to make it clear that he had nothing to do with the crime."

"Miss Duncan! Will you be staying in Owl Creek? Or have you decided to return to Florida?" a reporter called out.

Sage shifted from one foot to the next. The question was monumental. How was she supposed to answer it? Her birth family desperately wanted her to stick around town in order to get more acquainted with them. Eric had also urged her to stay in town, telling her she had twenty-five years to make up for with the Norths. The idea appealed to her, but she knew it would be agonizing to run into Hank knowing how he felt about her. She cringed just thinking about all the awkward run-ins and the regrets she would feel about keeping secrets from him. She'd decided to head home to Florida for a bit to heal her broken heart and get her bearings.

Before she could answer, there was a sudden commotion in the back of the crowd. Sage craned her neck to see who was pushing their way through. She must be a glutton for punishment because although it was silly of her to think Hank might grant her forgiveness, a part of her had hoped he would show up here today. Sage sighed. It was just another one of her pipe dreams.

Just then Hank appeared in the crowd, surrounded by Piper and Gabriel. Her heart began to thump wildly at the sight of him. The last few days without seeing him had felt like torture.

"Sage!" he called out. "I need to talk to you."

"Let her know how much you care about her," Gabriel yelled out.

"Tell her you were a fool!" Piper shouted.

The crowd erupted into laughter. Sage might have laughed too under other circumstances. She was standing as still as a statue, wondering what was coming next. Hank was a pretty private person. She couldn't imagine he wanted to put everything out there in front of the entire town of Owl Creek.

"Will you please be quiet?" Hank asked. "There are some things in life we need to do on our own steam. And this is one of them."

Beulah grabbed the microphone and said in a commanding voice, "Let the boy speak his piece." Her no-nonsense tone assured no argument. The queen of Owl Creek had spoken.

Hank's expression was sheepish. "Sorry about my timing, but as Mama always says, there's no perfect time to make things right. And I really want to make things right with you, Sage."

Eric gently nudged Sage forward. "Don't leave him hanging, sweetheart. I think he's pretty much wearing his heart on his sleeve at the moment." Sage stepped forward, her eyes focusing like laser beams on Hank. Suddenly her insides were doing crazy flip-flops. Was her father right about Hank? She'd practically given up all hope he'd come around, yet here he was trying to get her attention from deep in the crowd.

*Please, Lord. Let him have had a change of heart. Allow him to forgive me.*

Hank was rapidly making his way through the crowd and toward where she stood on the steps. The townsfolk made a wide path to allow him passage.

"Hank. What's going on? What are you doing here?" Sage whispered once he stood within mere feet of her. She looked around at all of the prying eyes. After all Hank had said to her the other day, he was the last person she'd expected to see today. Perhaps he had come to apologize so there would be no awkwardness between them. She knew he cared deeply for the North family, so it was a possible motive for his appearance at the press conference.

"Sage, I was wrong to come down so hard on you the other day. I acted like an idiot."

Just hearing those words allowed Sage to breathe properly for the first time in days. Her heart was pounding so loudly in her chest she feared Hank might hear it. She didn't need to say a word. All she wanted to do was listen to him. The sound of his voice was like a sweet melody.

"It shames me to face it, but it wounded my pride when I realized you hadn't trusted me enough to tell me why you came to Owl Creek. I told you about my past, so maybe you'll understand how I felt in that moment. I've been burnt before by believing in someone way more than they deserved. I thought I might be reliving that nightmare all over again. I should have listened to you rather than reacting from a place of hurt. It took me a few sleepless nights and some words of wisdom from the women in my family to make me see my own truths."

"And what are those truths?" Beulah asked. "Speak plainly, Sheriff."

Jennings stood beside his wife looking at Hank gruffly, as if he wasn't sure he was up to snuff for his granddaughter.

Sage couldn't help but grin at her grandmother's spunk. She'd asked the very question Sage wanted to inquire about herself. She would never get tired of learning more about the man she adored.

"The big one is that I love your granddaughter." He placed his hand over his heart. "I've fallen madly and deeply in love with her." He turned his gaze back toward Sage. "I have a question for you, Sage. Can you forgive a foolish sheriff for doubting you?"

For a moment Sage couldn't speak. She could barely think straight. The last few days had been a whirlwind of joy and the deepest sorrow she'd ever known. Against all hope, Hank was standing here offering her his heart. He was giving her way more than forgiveness. He was telling the whole entire town of Owl Creek that he loved her.

When she caught her breath, she was finally able to speak. "Oh, Hank! Of course I will. As long as you'll forgive me for not being truthful from the beginning. In case you didn't realize it, I'm crazy about you too. I don't know the precise moment when it happened, but you're firmly wedged in my soul."

A look of relief passed over his face. "I think my heart started to crack wide open that very first day on the ferry, and every day since then my feelings have increased by leaps and bounds. That big, beautiful heart of yours has taught me so much. Because of you my own has opened up so wide you could run a truck through it."

"Enough with all the talking. Seal it with a kiss," Beulah barked.

Hank and Sage burst into laughter. "Who am I to go against the grand dame of Owl Creek?" Hank asked as he lowered his head and placed a resounding kiss on Sage's lips. She reached up and placed her arms around Hank's neck and held on for dear life. Happiness fluttered through her at the realization that against all odds everything had come together with her birth family, the terrible secret she'd been harboring, and now, reuniting with Hank was the sweetest of blessings.

Even though they could hear the cameras snapping and lights flashing, they continued to share the most tender kiss of all time. She was home in Hank's loving embrace and it was the only place she wanted to be.

# Epilogue

"Miss Duncan. Miss Duncan." Sage felt a tugging sensation at the hem of her sweater.

When she looked down, Sage was staring into the deep brown eyes of one of her students, Charlie Miller. With a face full of freckles, and short, spiky hair, he was simply adorable And a bit on the mischievous side. Each and every day he kept Sage on her toes.

Charlie rubbed his hands together. "Are we doing show-and-tell soon?"

"As soon as your special guest arrives." She glanced up at the clock on the wall. "I hope they get here soon or we'll be behind schedule. Are you sure you don't want to tell me who's coming?"

Charlie shook his head. "Nope. It's a secret."

Second graders and their secrets!

Sage loved teaching second grade in Owl Creek. She was so incredibly blessed to be able to see these beautiful little faces every day and be their new teacher. Her class size was much smaller now and she truly felt as if she could give each child her very best. She loved her new life in Owl Creek with Hank and Addie and her wonderful birth family, the Norths. She was still getting to know them and trying to find her place in the family. She didn't expect it to happen all at once. It was a process, one that might take years to coalesce.

Her birth parents, Willa and Nate, were warm and generous people. They had showed Eric nothing but kindness and understanding. He'd been welcomed into the fold as if he were one of their own, and it made the entire situation so much easier to navigate. Now she had two dads! And she didn't have to worry about her father being prosecuted. She couldn't have asked for more.

Every Saturday she and Beulah met up at the teahouse for conversation and camaraderie.

Her grandmother was a hoot. She was teaching Sage so much about love and faith and their family. Although at first Sage had had to deal with a very guarded Connor, she had been able to peel back his layers to reveal a fiercely loyal and loving brother. Braden had been the biggest surprise of all. He'd come back to Owl Creek right after the truth about her identity was revealed. Right from the start he'd wrapped her up in a big bear hug and embraced her as his sister.

She let out a contented sigh. Everything had come together beautifully in the end. All her fears had been put to rest. All of a sudden Sage looked up and Hank was standing in the doorway of her classroom with Addie sitting on his hip. Her stomach did somersaults at the sight of him in his green winter parka and dark jeans. She quickly made her way to his side.

"Hank! What are you doing here?" she asked, concern ringing out in her voice. "Is everything all right with Addie? She's not sick, is she?" Sage reached out and pressed her palm against Addie's forehead. It felt as cool as ice.

"Addie isn't sick. She's right as rain."

Sage let out a relieved breath. "Okay. It's great to see the two of you, but I'm teaching right now. We're about to do show-and-tell. We have a special guest coming."

Hank grinned at her, sending butterflies soaring in her stomach. "I know. *I'm* the special guest."

She frowned at him, uncertain if she was being teased. "You are?"

He rocked back on his heels and gave her a smug look. "I sure am." He winked at her.

"Surprise!"

Sage felt flustered for a moment. She loved having Hank in her classroom, but she wasn't sure she would be able to concentrate due to his close proximity. He made her feel almost dizzy with happiness. She couldn't even put into words the unbridled joy he'd brought into her life. Her life had truly changed by coming to Owl Creek!

"Hey there! Most of you know me. I'm Hank Crawford, town sheriff. And this is my daughter, Addie. First, let me tell you how fortunate you are to have Miss Duncan as your teacher."

"She's real pretty," chirped Suzie Walters.

"And nice!" Charlie chimed in.

"She's both of those things and more," Hank responded. "She's transformed this town in ways that are too huge to put into words. She gave us all hope when some of us had stopped believing. Miss Duncan has healed a lot of hearts, including my own."

Sage felt a tear trickle down her face. Addie reached up and tried to wipe it away. Sage leaned down and placed a kiss on her temple.

Hank reached for Sage's free hand. He entwined it with his own and dropped down on bended knee. Sage let out a gasp. Before she knew what was happening, a beaming Trudy came in and scooped Addie up in her arms, then stepped to the side.

"Thanks, Mama," Hank said before turning his focus back to Sage. "Before you came into my life I was determined to keep my heart hardened to the possibility of falling in love again. You showed me that taking leaps of faith is what we're supposed to do in this lifetime. God wants us to love one another. And I do love you, Sage Duncan." He took both of her hands and lifted them to his mouth for a kiss. "I want to treasure you for the rest of our days. I want to grow old with you. I want to have snowball fights with you and walk hand in hand every year on the owl walk trail. I want you to be Addie's mother and show her what it means to be a caring, loving woman of faith. Sage, will you marry us? Will you be my wife and Addie's mother?"

Sage wanted to pinch herself. Was this really happening? It was like something out of her most precious dreams.

She let out the breath she'd been holding. "Of course I will, Hank. I can't think of a more blissful way to spend the rest of my life than with you and Addie," Sage said, burrowing herself against Hank's chest as the children in the classroom began to hoot and holler.

"Oops. I almost forgot the ring." Hank reached into his jacket pocket and pulled out a cedar box. He lifted the lid to reveal a round diamond with smaller stones surrounding it.

"It's beautiful," Sage whispered, holding out her ring finger so Hank could slide it on.

"Not half as lovely as you are," Hank said, leaning in to place a celebratory kiss on his fiancée's lips.

"Oh, Hank. Thank you for changing my life. Not only am I going to be your wife, but I'm going to be Addie's mother. I came to Owl Creek to find answers about my birth family, but I found so much more. I found you. And Addie. And my birthright. And a town full of people I adore. I couldn't ask for more, Hank. God has been so good to me."

"Neither can I, sweetheart. You made me believe in love again. And happy endings. I'll always be grateful to you for bringing my heart back to life."

Sage beamed at Hank. Never in a million years had she imagined this blissful ending. Her entire being was filled with love and gratitude. "As long as we're together I'll have a joyful heart," Sage said, wrapping her arms around Hank's neck and pulling him toward her so she could place a tender kiss on his lips.

"We are blessed beyond measure. I can't wait for you to become my Owl Creek bride," Hank said, his voice full of love and a deep certainty that foreshadowed their amazing future.

"I'm finally home, Hank," Sage murmured, wiping away a tear. "Right where I was meant to be all along."

\* \* \* \* \*

Dear Reader,

Thank you for joining me on this new journey to Owl Creek, Alaska. I really enjoyed writing Hank and Sage's love story. I hope you loved it, as well.

Writing this book was a labor of love and it challenged me in ways I haven't been challenged before.

From the moment Sage steps onto the page she is a woman with a huge dilemma. She can either lay claim to her legacy as Lily North or protect the man who raised her. Her loyalty is inspiring.

Hank is a caring man and a loving father who wants to live his life with honor and integrity. Having been burned before in a relationship, he isn't sure he wants to love again. Until Sage comes into his life. Both characters are incredible people who are better together than apart. For me, that's the crux of it.

Although Hank and Sage are the hero and heroine, Jane's actions set the story in motion.

Throughout the book I kept asking myself the question: Why would a woman steal another woman's baby? To me, it's inconceivable. Yet the North family forgave Jane and granted her grace. Astounding, right? So many times we let bitterness triumph over forgiveness.

God's command is to love another, a theme that resonates throughout the book. Love is everywhere in Owl Creek!

I truly appreciate you spending some time reading *Her Secret Alaskan Family* and meeting this cast of characters!

Blessings,
*Belle*

# WE HOPE YOU ENJOYED THIS BOOK!

*Love Inspired*

New beginnings. Happy endings. Discover uplifting inspirational romance.

Look for six new Love Inspired books available every month, wherever books are sold!

*Could this bad-boy newcomer spell trouble for an Amish spinster...or be the answer to her prayers?*

*Read on for a sneak preview of*
An Unlikely Amish Match,
*the next book in Vannetta Chapman's miniseries*
Indiana Amish Brides.

The sun was low in the western sky by the time Micah Fisher hitched a ride to the edge of town. The driver let him out at a dirt road that led to several Amish farms. He'd never been to visit his grandparents in Indiana before. They always came to Maine. But he had no trouble finding their place.

As he drew close to the lane that led to the farmhouse, he noticed a young woman standing by the mailbox. A little girl was holding her hand and another was hopping up and down. They were all staring at him.

"Howdy," he said.

The woman only nodded, but the two girls whispered, "Hello."

"Can we help you?" the woman asked. "Are you...lost?"

"*Nein*. At least I don't think I am."

"You must be if you're here. This is the end of the road."

Micah pointed to the farm next door. "Abigail and John Fisher live there?"

"They do."

"Then I'm not lost." He snatched off his baseball cap, rubbed the top of his head and then yanked the cap back on.

Micah stepped forward and held out his hand. "I'm Micah—Micah Fisher. Pleased to meet you."

"You're not *Englisch*?"

"Of course I'm not."

LIEXP0120

"So you're Amish?" She stared pointedly at his clothing—tennis shoes, blue jeans, T-shirt and baseball cap. Pretty much what he wore every day.

"I'm as Plain and simple as they come."

"I somehow doubt that."

"Since we're going to be neighbors, I suppose I should know your name."

"Neighbors?"

"*Ja.* I've come to live with my *daddi* and *mammi*—at least for a few months. My parents think it will straighten me out." He peered down the lane. "I thought the bishop lived next door."

"He does."

"Oh. You're the bishop's *doschder*?"

"We all are," the little girl with freckles cried. "I'm Sharon and that's Shiloh and that is Susannah."

"Nice to meet you, Sharon and Shiloh and Susannah."

Sharon lost interest and squatted to pick up some of the rocks. Shiloh hid behind her *schweschder*'s skirt, and Susannah scowled at him.

"I knew the bishop lived next door, but no one told me he had such pretty *doschdern*."

Susannah's eyes widened even more, but it was Shiloh who said, "He just called you pretty."

"Actually I called you all pretty."

Shiloh ducked back behind Susannah.

Susannah narrowed her eyes as if she was squinting into the sun, only she wasn't. "Do you talk to every girl you meet that way?"

"Not all of them—no."

*Don't miss*
An Unlikely Amish Match *by Vannetta Chapman,*
*available February 2020 wherever*
*Love Inspired*® *books and ebooks are sold.*

LoveInspired.com